SHOELESS

Shoeless

A novel

Carol Ann DeLaRosa

Library of Congress Cataloging-in-Publication Data available.
DeLaRosa, Carol Ann.
Shoeless / Carol Ann DeLaRosa

ISBN 979-8-218-04408-4
1.Romance-Fiction. 2.Thrillers Suspense-Fiction

Printed in the United States of America on acid free paper.

Lulu Publishing   Lulu.com

Cover design with *Canva.*

Cover photograph by Pete Johnson

My husband is constantly telling me that I "overthink" things. Bless his heart! Well, not today. I'm revealing all of the events that happened, just as they occurred over the past six months. All of this took place in the blink of an eye. I'm writing this to you as quickly as I can and as well as I remember. You can be the judge. You know how to find me.

As my journey begins, I am driving towards the McDonald's behind Crabtree Valley Mall, in Raleigh, and I hear the radio announcer proclaim, "Caller nine wins the new Les Miserables, the movie! Call now!" Granted, the prize was just a DVD, but

I really liked the film when we saw it last Christmas. As an "Extreme Couponer," I look at this opportunity as one less item to purchase. However, as a self-proclaimed semi-professional radio contest winner, dating back to my junior high days in South Florida with Y-100, a DVD wasn't that great of a prize. Long ago, my brother and I would win everything…at least once a month and sometimes multiple times for the same prize. From album collections, movie tickets, Disney World tickets, Six Flags Atlantis packs, cash, and much more.

Then one day, before Clear Channel Corporation Radio days, they changed their policy. You could only win once per household every thirty days. Unfortunately, you can partially thank us for this rule. So, I was back into winning a lot last year when all of the movie premiere passes came out on various radio stations: The Avengers, MIB3, The Heat etc. I won all of them. My greatest prize was when Randi West on G-105 gave away $1,000 when she said the secret word during the five o'clock hour a few holidays ago.

SHOELESS

I pull off to the side of the road to call in. I tell myself, "Cat, what have you got to lose?" I never dial the phone while driving anymore, since my best friend Charlotte was hit by a driver that was texting a few years ago, and now doesn't have full use of her legs. The phone is ringing! I win! I remind myself that I must remember this date, because I can't win again on this station for thirty more days, but after today's memorable events, this will definitely not be a problem.

It was a gorgeous, bright, sunny, but cool, end of March morning, 2013. Maybe it wasn't the actual day, which happens to be Holy Thursday, but the fact was that I had the day off of work! I need a little break. Granted, my job with this family has offered me a lot: happiness, laughter, adventure, and a great reason to get up and enjoy life!

Since I closed my photography studio last year, I've been, let's say, depressed. I had no job. No purpose. Funny how my college-age daughter helped me turn my life around. After I was sitting around and doing nothing, except for gaining

3

weight, she told me I would make a great nanny. She had been one over the summer, and said I did a great job raising her and her three brothers, plus deep down I missed the craziness and loudness of little ones, so I should apply.

At first, I was apprehensive. Yes, I did have four children in six years, and my baby was now starting college, but what skills did I have? Actually, I possess a lot of skills for this job. Plus, this time, unlike raising my own children, I would get a good night's sleep, which never happened when my own were little. I think I was a zombie for the first ten years; Sleep deprived, I rarely showered, you know. But I was skilled. Cooking, cleaning, breaking up arguments among siblings, chauffeuring, homework...you know the endless list.

I remember Ann Landers had put an actual salary on mothering duties. Not that I would be someone else's mother, but I am great at "Love and Hugs." I put a salary plus benefits package out there, and after just one interview, I got a nanny job! It was to start at the end of last summer to four children;

from ten to one year old. ALL BOYS! I think they also hired me because the mom thought I was a devout Catholic. I am sure that their definition of "devout" and mine are different. But yes, I am, and always have been a practicing Catholic. I'm really not sure what that means, as I follow most of the "rules." (If I kept up with no birth control, I'd have twenty kids by now. No thank you!). I am also going through some personal spiritual difficulties in trying to understand God and all. I don't get it.

It's been an adventurous seven months. This family loves to travel, and I get to go with them. I went to a water park, down a three-story waterslide with one of the kids. I held him so tight, screaming all the way down the slide. He just laughed and laughed. I was the one screaming. This little guy tells everyone that Miss Cathy was a "scaredy-cat."

It's funny how I never would have done this with my own kids when they were little. You can say I was overprotective. Just ask any of them. Oh, how the new "Miss Cathy" has changed. The quiet caterpillar has finally turned into a confident butterfly, flying coast to coast.

I decided to spend the beginning part of this day catching up with my dearest and closest friend Charlotte. Unlike myself, she stayed in the photography business. I give her credit.

As the new digital world encircled us, complete with cameras on our phones, everyone seems to be a "professional photographer." The new photography world is, simply put, idiotic. We will see in future generations how families today took crappy photographs, let alone portraits. Lighting, posing, and even clothes and colors made a difference in portraits. Everyone now considers themselves a "professional" because they think it's the camera, not the skill. Along with overdone retouching, no one looks like themselves after retouching here, there, and everywhere!

Even though I am no longer photographing for a living, I tell everyone to hire a professional and get your family photographed every few years. Time is precious, don't worry about your weight issues (that was the number one excuse for not being in a portrait), and invest in this priceless gift. You never know who may not be with you when you are finally "ready."

Okay, I'll get off of my soapbox. That profession, of fifteen years, gave me a great house and a good living before it tanked. Believe it or not, all I wanted to be was a fashion photographer, fly around the world, photograph for a crazy amount of money, and come home until the next assignment. I never ended up there, but instead was your local family and children's photographer.

I had all of the business trappings of day-to-day operations: filing too much paperwork, keeping employees happy, keeping clients happy, trying to find time for my own family, trying to continually find new clients, actual photographing, checking inventory, marketing, social media posts, updating the daily blog, and finally falling behind in taxes. I'm very behind in past due taxes with tons of penalties and interest payments. Even though the business closed, I still owe the government.

SHOELESS

Back to what happened with my lunch with Char. Can you tell I have ADHD? I'm trying to stick to my point, but my mind is full! There is so much you need to know, and very little time.

SHOELESS

"I Knew You Were Trouble
When You Walked In"
-Taylor Swift, Trouble

Charlotte and I finally meet up at the McDonald's. I haven't been in one of these "establishments," rather, "Fast Food Restaurants" since the last calendar year, a whole three months ago, as I have been trying to lose weight with Weight Watchers. Every "point" I eat or drink is precious to me! I never made myself and my health a priority until this year. I order a grilled chicken sandwich, small salad and toss half of the bun. Over fifteen pounds lost so far and counting! I even wore my long-sleeved UNC t-shirt without a hoodie over it, just to see if Char would notice. She did, immediately! She still has the perfect figure.

It's sad that it's been months since we've had lunch together. In my business days, we made a point of it almost every other week. Now with this new job, I don't get much time off during the week.

As we start gabbing, I look up and see a man walk in. We make quick eye contact. He's taller than 6 feet, rugged, muscular, not quite clean shaven, wearing a dark leather bomber jacket and cap to match, with amazing dark hair with a hint of gray. Something is so familiar about him. Do I know him? Possibly.

After being in Raleigh for 25 years, was he someone from church, a past client, maybe a parent of one of my kids' friends? Boy, that can be even harder: was he from one of their schools, sports teams, dance classes, art school? I can't remember.

Char and I catch up on our lives. The kids, husbands, work and fun are discussed. As usual, both of our husbands are away too much. Mine is a Physician's Assistant and is volunteering at a medical mission in Mexico for the week. Hers is a social worker in Chapel Hill.

SHOELESS

Ron and Char have been married five years longer than us, and we met when our husbands were little league coaches for our oldest children when they were five, over twenty years ago.

Most of the time our conversations are about the same things. Not much changes. Our lives are fine, nothing exciting to talk about. We have nothing to complain about either. We are blessed with loving and faithful husbands, healthy young adult children, stable jobs, enough food to eat, and lovely homes each designed with old, early attic style furniture. (Yes, everything needs to be replaced). We are both "Flybaby's" (from the "FlyLady," who helps people with housekeeping routines) and are trying to keep our homes clean and organized. I think she is struggling with this challenge more than me. However, now we don't have the photography business in common anymore. I am still interested, though. I remind her that when that fashion shoot arises and she has to travel to think of me! Yes, she knows of this dream of mine. She would joke, calling our new company "Hire the Handicapped."

SHOELESS

As we start to feast on our ever so "'healthy lunches" I explain my latest trip last week with my Nanny Family to Naples, Florida. From the silly things like the TSA having to "pat me down" at the airport because I had on a hoodie, and being told that the hoodie was way too big for me! I took it as a compliment and told them I was losing weight.

I can never go into too much detail about the family I work for, since I signed several confidentiality forms. But I can say some of my adventures without giving names. I spoke about last week, oh, it was at their Florida house that we stayed, rather a mansion, two stories high in every room and surveillance cameras inside! I once wished to be in a house like this. Rather, I got my wish, however, I was "working" and not owning this house. So, be careful how you phrase your wishes! I also took the kids in their infinity pool. First time I swam in one of those! Funny thing, a tourist cruise came by in the canal in their backyard. The kids made funny faces, waved and laughed at the people on the boat. This happened a few times on the trip.

They are fun and funny boys! The cruises around the neighborhood reminded me of what you would see on Lifestyles of the Rich and Famous, as they tell you who lives at which mansion. The grandfather told his grandsons not to look at the boats, as they could end up in a tabloid. I knew then that I should have worn a better swimsuit (Yes, this is a famous family!).

I told Char about the Naples Zoo and the kids and the mom riding on the camel. I decided to stay off of the camel and stay with the baby and the grandma. Though I could write chapters about each member of this family, I will share one special member with you. Let me explain about Grandma: she is an exquisite and fit European woman, say in her late fifties, who has traveled the world many times. She is active (bicycling and tennis), I wish I had her figure and stamina. She has been in the company of heads of state, countries, and more CEOs than I can name. She is genuinely a nice lady and doesn't treat me like "the hired help." Actually no one in the family does. I explain to Charlotte that as the family is riding around on the camel at the zoo, I simply ask Grandma, "Have you ever been on a camel?"

And she responded in her accent, so matter-of-factly: "Oh yes…I think the last time was in Saudi Arabia." But, of course, Saudi Arabia! I laugh inside. This was the closest I've ever been to a camel! I pause and eat some of my lunch.

"I'm from Saudi Arabia," says the dark-haired mystery man in a deep, sexy voice, who now is sitting at the table next to Char and me. I didn't notice his presence. I had been so absorbed in our girl talk that everything and everyone else was oblivious to me.

Char responds "Oh, nice." I had barely heard his response, so didn't even chime in to the comment. I was so focused on my conversation with Char that he honestly wasn't on my radar. Char kept turning her head to watch him after that comment.

We finished and got up from our little table. As I stood, the man took my hand and said, with his accent, "You're a beautiful woman. May I have your telephone number?"

As I pulled my hand away from his, I responded, "Thank you, but no. I am happily married." Ooooh, I could feel shivers, worse than goose bumps, almost an electrical surge, go through my body. I looked into his eyes. Something still seemed familiar, yet distant.

Char and I left quickly and started walking to our cars. "That was just weird," I said.

And Char, who is the comedic of the two of us, quickly came back with, "He probably needs a green card."

SHOELESS

"You Don't Know You're Beautiful"
-One Direction, <u>What Makes You Beautiful</u>

I started the car and just sat for a moment. This man out of nowhere called me beautiful! Green Card seeker or not, it was nice to hear. Don't get me wrong, but after being married forever, well, almost thirty years, I guess my husband doesn't quite use that term often. He compliments me when we go out, as in "Cat, you look nice," but I can't remember the last time he said "beautiful." Wow, how a word can change the way you feel. Someone other than my husband thinks that I am beautiful! Yes, I know, just a pickup line, but a great one at that.

This man with the accent seemed so familiar. Still can't place him.

SHOELESS

My cell phone rang. I love that ringtone. I am hearing the bell tower chimes, just like those we heard when we were on our honeymoon in Europe. I stopped the engine, looked down at the phone to see the "Love of My Life" and answered it to the sound of my loving husband's voice. "Hi Honey!" I was trying to remember, was he two hours ahead, or two hours behind? Either way, it's still daytime in Mexico.

"Staying out of trouble my love?" he asks. Matt is always funny that way, as he knows that I spend five days a week keeping four little boys busy. How much "trouble" could I get into? He's a pure Latino, though he was born in America, as were his parents. Latin men have a tendency to be very jealous and very passionate. Combine that with marrying me, a redhead. Watch out! Tempers can flare!

Did he know I had today off to start my Easter week? He usually calls me on a Sunday. I replied with a goofy answer, "Well, an Arabian man just told me I was beautiful and wanted my number

17

inside the Mickey D's when I was having lunch with Char."

Yup, it was indeed a goofy answer, to which Matt replied, "He must be in search of a Green Card. Now if you were in a fancy restaurant and this happened, I might get suspicious."

The Green Card answer wins, again, but it was still nice to hear. I did find out that the Love of My Life will be returning on the Saturday afternoon flight, so we will have time to attend the Easter Vigil that evening at church. This is the first year that we won't be at the beach for Easter week, since most of our kids can't be home. That's okay with me, as we can have a great week together. I have all of next week off!

Maybe we can discuss our finances and see where we are. There is so much to fix up or replace on our fifteen-year-old house. Plus, I still owe the government a boatload of money for taxes I didn't pay while I was in business. (Money I chose to use to feed my family rather than send to the government, as times were tough. I know, I chose incorrectly, and have a huge penalty. The business was changing those last few years.) The taxes, health bills, and more need to be addressed. Now that I have a regular paycheck, which honestly didn't occur during the last few years in business, we can fix some issues…and maybe the oven!

When I say he is a physician's assistant, I must add that Matt works at a nonprofit and makes a lot less than one in the regular field. We have never been "rich." Just rich in love and happiness. Cheesy, I know. Believe it or not, we are still the best of friends. I could call him my "soul mate," however, I decide not to, as that terminology wasn't around when we met, so he's simply "The Love of My Life."

We met in 1986. I was eighteen, in my second semester in college, and he was twenty-two, and we are still very much in love. (Simple coincidence is that he has the same first name as my high school sweetheart.) He is a good, honest, caring, loving person to everyone. I trust him with my life. It's others that I don't always trust around him (I watch too many Lifetime movies. They are true to life, you know!).

But as I have repeated to him through the years, "If you want someone else, just let me know."

Of course, he thinks I'm kidding, and his set response is "You're it, kid, for our lifetime. I vowed to you!" I believe that I am a confident, and "now" beautiful (according to green card man) forty-five-year-old that stayed at home when the kids were little, watched every "Oprah" and "The View" episode that I could videotape. Add the knowledge I gained with each motivational-self-help-spiritual book that Oprah touted about self-esteem, money, inner beauty and peace, along with her Book Club. Add laughing with "Ellen" a few years later. I'm a real woman, ready to fight for her man, funny. If not, I will survive!

Matt and I don't really fight. At least I can't remember the last argument. He's true to me, as I am to him. Well, pretty much, as I am a "good Catholic wife." Our relationship must seem strange to the world, as most couples don't last as long as we have. We must seem pretty boring to the outside world. Sure, it's not always easy. We are not perfect people. Now that our fourth baby has flown the coop, we are reconnecting. We have too much invested in each other. We have our hearts along with a lot of debt. Debt is our topic of contention.

This isn't easy, being apart, though. He just returned from helping people in the slums of New York City for a few weeks, then I went to Naples, Florida, for a week, and he's been in Mexico for a week and a half volunteering his medical services. He hinted that he might be going back regularly to set up their new medical clinics. Before this year, we were hardly ever apart. We enjoy spending time together. And yes, we are still very passionate with one another.

Somehow it all works. I have a few days to prepare for his homecoming. It was great to hear my husband's voice, even only for a few minutes. Now onto the events of the rest of my day.

Driving home alone is always fun for me. I blast the radio and sing! I have a lousy singing voice compared to just about anyone, especially my family of singers. I can't hold a note, but I have freedom in my car, to be as loud and way off key as I want.

As I pull into the garage, an old "Journey" song comes on and it all comes back to me. Oh, my goodness!

SHOELESS

"One night will remind you..."
-Journey, Separate Ways

I had just graduated from a "good Catholic high school" in Boca Raton, Florida, Class of 1985. An honor roll student, and a good/nice girl image. My parents wouldn't let me go on the "Official Senior Cruise" because all they saw was too much partying with fellow classmates. Nevertheless, my Aunt Sarah and her best friend since grade school, Tess (I call her Aunt Tess) asked my mom if I could join them on a cruise to the Bahamas after graduation. Yes! Freedom! I know they only wanted me so they could split the room cost three ways, as it was the same price for two, three, or four, in a room. Whatever...a five-day cruise to the Bahamas!

SHOELESS

Having only watched "The Love Boat" growing up, I guess I didn't realize a few things about my first cruise. First, the rooms are small, and the bathrooms are even smaller. It was nothing like "The Love Boat." Well, at least not our room. We had two bunk style beds, connected to the wall, and barely enough room to sit down in the bathroom. Add on "the drill" with the sirens, we all have to run up to the deck and put on life vests. The first day was pretty much shot with this drill.

All you can eat and drink. I'm not sure if that's alcohol, but I'll pass. Did I mention that I won't be 18 for two more months, and the drinking age is 19, soon to be changed to 21 in Florida and across the country? I can still eat like a pig and not gain an ounce. I need to appreciate this as I hear and see those around me that are older in different shapes.

The first night was fun, as I hung around my "aunts." We walked around a lot and caught a movie. Yup, a movie on a cruise! My aunts decided they want me to call them only by their first names on this cruise. I said I would oblige if she would stop calling me Catherine on this trip. I always thought it sounded too stuffy. Tess laughed and said "Catie is your new name. Just don't do anything that I'd have to explain to your mother."

Tess was single and fifteen years older than me. Could my "Good Girl Aunt" want to get lucky on this trip? She can have all the fun she wants. I'm here to "see the world," even though it's pretty much in my Palm Beach County backyard, I've never been anywhere except to see my grandparents in New York. Plus, I have a tan, blonde, hot lifeguard of a boyfriend back home. I don't need or want anyone else. Just me and my Nikon FE-2 and I'll be happy.

The second day was spent on deck at the pool. Having shoulder-length strawberry blonde curly hair, I basically go from "translucent" in color to "lobster red" in the sun. So, I stayed in the shade, with a hat and lots of suntan lotion! I had a stack of Teen, Seventeen, Glamour, and Vogue, and snuck the latest issue of Cosmopolitan magazine from my mom's room to keep me company. I wish Vogue would have a teen issue, as the styles are different from what teens wear. But when I'm an "adult" I can wear these clothes. (When exactly are you an adult?) I had a soda that certainly tasted different on the cruise ship, especially with a fancy shaped glass with an umbrella in it. I told my aunt, rather "Sarah" and "Tess," that the waiter was sure asking us if we need anything a lot. Tess laughs and replies, "Catie, he's hitting on you!" Seriously? Not interested. Tess tells me to loosen up, that's a "Catherine" attitude. "Catie" is here now.

We had a late dinner seating, and then went back to change our clothes. Tess gave me a dress she brought for herself tonight. Apparently, a "Catie" dress. Low cut in the front and back, short and sexy. It was neon yellow, but it is a Bahama trip. I've never worn anything like this. Even at Prom Night a few weeks ago, we wore white, long, poufy dresses with lace. This was an "adult dress." Sarah was okay with this, reminding me of my blonde hunk Matthew back home and his 18th birthday party this coming weekend. What trouble could I get into?

It was now after ten, or maybe even eleven, when we got to the dance club. Sarah and Tess like to gamble, so it took a while to get to the club. It was loud, with colorful disco lights all over. People jumping up and down. I hope my parts stay in this dress if I jump!

We danced the night away and had so much fun! We were out until past two a.m.

*

The next day we got to visit the island. Those CRAZY taxi drivers!

I went into my first ever casino. They had just installed new slot machines so I guess people didn't realize that when you win, you now have to press another button to collect your winnings. Sarah and Tess sat and dropped quarters, but I walked around and picked up other peoples' winnings that were left inside abandoned machines. I presented my bucket for paper money and hopes that I didn't get carded. I don't know if there is a legal gambling age. Total: $69!

After a few hours, we walked around the town and heard beautiful music, like the calypso version of Red, Red, Wine, on the side of the street. We also saw Christopher Columbus's official statue. It wasn't a long day on the island, but a fun one. Back to eat again, dance some more, and go to the midnight buffet. What elaborate ice sculptures, in many shapes and sizes.

*

The next morning, I slept in and found a note on the mirror. 'Back at the pool. See you up on deck.'

Somehow, I made to it to the pool deck, seeing Tess and Sarah at a table laughing with two men. Hesitant to approach them, I stare from afar. Sarah sees me and waves me over. I am introduced to Zaran and Mehmet, who just happen to be brothers. They are both hot, and I don't catch the name that belongs to each of them. They are older than me, but younger than "my non-aunts." I slowly walk over and join them.

I find out that they are from Saudi Arabia, work with something about oil, attending graduate school in Texas and are here on this cruise on a break. I just graduated from high school and don't know a thing about Saudi Arabia. Is that where the women are completely covered, including their hair, or the place where there are harems? (Was that where all the weird sexual things occur with a lot of women and one wealthy man? Or did I read it incorrectly in my mom's magazine a few months ago?)

I calculated that graduate school makes them at least 23 years old. Too old for me, way too young for my aunts. (Plus, I am not interested, as I am already quite happy with my lifeguard back home.) After about an hour, I excuse myself and start to walk around the deck. I hope my aunts have fun. That one brother, though, has captivating eyes. And a heck of a body. And the accent, I heard more

Spanish than Saudi, but I don't really know what it is supposed to sound like. Maybe that's their accent.

I didn't get far when I hear a version of "Catie" with an absolutely deep, strong, gorgeous accent. I didn't remember the name of this man; was he Mehmet or Zaran? "Catie, wait up!" I didn't understand that he even said "Catie" at first, as it sounded like "Caught-ee" in his accent. I turn around and he handed me my Swatch. It was one of the brothers. THAT brother! God, he was good looking. Magical eyes. "You left your watch on the table."

"It's a Swatch," I reply. Yes, I took it off at the table as to not get a weird sunburn on my wrist.

"Oh, I have a Rolex on," he said so nonchalantly. He must be an Arabian Sheikh. I feel like a pauper as he hands me my red, yellow and blue piece of plastic. Note to self: throw this watch out. This says high school, not college girl. It's been four days since I graduated high school, thus making me an official college student.

"Well, thanks. You can go back to…" Oh, I couldn't say my aunt and her friend, I just kind of pointed in their direction.

He asks me, "Why? You don't want to be seen in my presence?" I giggle. Was he serious? Oh, that accent makes me weak all over, forget just the knees!

How do I play this? Play? What am I thinking? Well, this is a cruise, I'll never see him again, I am now the new Catie. We only have two days left. I'm getting ahead of myself. He's just talking with me. "Let's get in the shade. Would you like a drink?" He did just ask me if I wanted a drink, and I don't think it's soda.

"Sure," I try to think of the name of something alcoholic. I decided I didn't do the whole drunken weekend party group in high school, because I saw my parents drink too much. Plus, I want to stay in control of my thoughts and actions. As I think about all of the liquor bottles in the "official liquor cabinet" at my parents' house, "Mimosa, please" I request. Hopefully the bartender will go heavy on the orange juice. As I select a covered area to lounge, he pulls out the chair for me. A gentleman! A gorgeous Arabian gentleman. Man, Catherine, I mean Catie! Still not remembering which brother I was with; he went to get us drinks. I gob on tons of suntan lotion.

Before we drink, he raises his glass to toast to something. As I raise mine, he proclaims, "To a beautiful beginning of a lifetime of adventure." As our glasses touched, my mind went racing. What did he just say? Lifetime? Adventure?

After some conversation, he mentions Mehmet by name, which means he is Zaran! I immediately ask, "Zaran is an interesting name."

"My real name is Hazar. Zar was a nickname until later in college when my roommate mentioned the comic book character named Zaran. Hence, Zaran I became." I don't follow comics, so I was thinking, "Whatever!"

I must have looked confused, as he then pulled out his green passport and opened it to show me his name. All I saw was a man in a turban and a city that started with the letter D. He said he was born there, but raised in boarding schools in Spain. Hence, the Spanish-like mixed Arabic accent. I also found out that his brother's real name is Muhammed, but they call him Mehmet. Well, I'm really Catherine, but Catie this week! (I was too embarrassed to tell him I was named after a soap opera character my mom liked.)

He also told me that he noticed me dancing last night. Oh no, then I told him a little white lie. Not straight out, just when he asked if I was finishing college soon, I said I had a couple of years to go in Miami. I think he thought I went to the University of Miami, but I didn't correct him, since I will be a freshman at a little Catholic college in Miami.

Why am I here with this man? I could so get into trouble with him. I knew that as soon as I laid eyes on him. This is not me. But who am I, a confused seventeen-year-old, pretending to have her twenty-first birthday in a few months? I can pretend. For two days. Unless of course, my aunts say something. But they looked interested in pursuing the brothers. Oh, am I going to be in trouble!

We talked for hours, but it went by so quickly. He was mesmerizing. We shared about everything that seemed important in my life and future. We had this immediate connection that I never felt with anyone. I told him that I wanted to be a fashion photographer who jet sets out for an assignment and still comes home to a bunch of little ones by the end of the day. Plus make a crazy amount of money.

He asked me what my travel plans were. I didn't have any. I quickly thought about it and said I'd love to go to Italy and maybe the Alps one day. Even live there, maybe on a lake somewhere. Well, a girl can dream!

Zaran said he could give me the world. I thought he was joking until he said he was pursuing an international law degree. I see money in that profession! Oh, I could see us together. My parents though? Once I tell them he is Non-Catholic, let alone Arab…I could push the lawyer idea…what am I thinking? I just met this man a few hours ago, but we had this magnetic force, and I know he could feel it too.

Crap. Reality hits, I have my high school sweetheart teenage boyfriend back in Boca that really loves me. I could see me with Matthew, my tall, tanned, Caucasian lifeguard forever too. I am so confused.

It was time to dress for dinner. I got up slowly from the pool chair thinking; I definitely have red stripes on my thighs and lower back from sitting on this chair too long. There I go again; I have some problem with thinking too many things at once. I wonder if there's a pill for that problem. I stand with indented stripes, put a towel around my bottom half, and thanked him for a nice afternoon. He stood and put his arms around my back, touching my towel. With chills vibrating throughout me, he looked deep in my eyes, "You're a beautiful woman. Save me a dance later tonight." Breathless, *like ya know,* really? I had never been called those words before:

beautiful and a woman! Then he held my hand and walked me to my hallway

＊

After a few hours, the ladies arrived back in our walk-in closet sized room. Tess immediately declared, "Catie, you hit the jackpot!"

Sarah, however, wasn't so optimistic. "He's closer to our age then you. Plus, you have…"

"STOP!" I begin as she started to say Matthew's name. "You two are sending me such mixed signals! Wear a sexy dress, drop the "Aunt" in your names, this, that, how about this. Tomorrow when we get off of the ship, and I just want to go sightseeing on my own. A photographic adventure for me. That's what I want! You two don't have to babysit me. Go do something crazy. Win your jackpot! Earlier today was just a drink with this guy. Nothing else. You know who I am!"

Just as those words came out, I really began to think. Who am I? Catherine was the good little Catholic girl that obeys all of the rules, listens to her parents, honor roll student, and has Catholic guilt about everything. Is this what happens as you grow up? Or am I just crazy? I'll be out of my parents' house in a few months, have this summer available for fun with my friends in Boca, and then start college. It's not excessive drinking; I don't want to be like my parents. But what is it? I'm a good person, basically. Caring, giving, loving, and faithful. Catherine for almost 18 years...who is Catie? Today, she became deeply attracted to a much older man. Yes, she did. I mean, I did.

*

The three of us had another fun evening. After dinner, the cruise director, Julie (funny coincidence) announced the different excursions and shows available on the island tomorrow. We decided they could pick a show and then I could venture off like a "Big Girl" and do my own thing. I just wanted to photograph.

We went around the ship, visited the duty-free shops, then the aunts gambled again (not me, I work too hard at Eckerd's for $3.35 an hour to want to lose it), and finally we went dancing at ten (no one was there before then).

We danced together. Then they danced with other men. As I returned to the dance floor, I felt a hand wrap around my waist. As I turned, he squeezed harder, pushed me closer and kissed me! Hard! Right there on the dance floor! I hope my aunts didn't see this. Nope. They were dancing with other guys across the room. I pushed away and shouted "What was that?" An Arabian greeting...on the lips? A marking of one's territory? Here I go again, over thinking. But he did smell good. So good.

I'm not grown up enough for this. I said goodnight to Zaran after the song, told my aunts that I was going to the all-night buffet.

As I was in the hall, Zaran followed me and took my hand and we walked on deck. Damn, this was too romantic. The moonlight, stars, and cool breeze. He wanted to know what was wrong. He said he waited all day for tonight. I apologized if he thought that I was leading him on earlier. I explained that I wasn't looking for a one-night stand. I just left it at that. I needed to go to my cubbyhole of a room to think. Alone.

Zaran kissed my cheek and asked if he could see me on the island. I said I didn't know. All I wanted was to clear my head and photograph the sites tomorrow. He said, "You and I are meant to be together forever. You can feel it. It's not just a pickup line, my Catie. It's in our souls. Remember this date: Wednesday, May 22, 1985."

Souls? I haven't heard that word since the Rod Stewart song that was our prom theme a few weeks ago. Lord, I am so confused. I did just meet this man today, right?

*

The next day, my aunts and I made it to the island and show alive. It is not leaving the cruise ship and going onto a smaller boat to the island. It's the taxi! I swear these taxi drivers are still trying to kill us! Swerving all around the streets.

We entered a casino that had an auditorium in the back. As the lights went out, guess who sits next to me? Seriously? And his brother sat next to him. How did he know where I'd be? It's dark; he whispers in my ear, "Did you bring your camera?" What exactly did that mean? The music to the magic show begins.

Zaran places his hand on the side of my thigh. Wait! What the hell did these ladies get us tickets to? A group of long legged, beautiful women step out on stage with their backs to the audience, wearing the highest of heels, fishnet stockings, sequined bikini bottoms (at least a string) filled with feathers flowing behind them, huge glitzy hats, and colorful feather boas covering their backs with their arms. Were we in Vegas? Oh no. They turned around and all you saw were the boas now covering their breasts. The dancers put one arm up and then the other. Forget about a fancy costume in the front and all you see are bare breasts. All shapes and sizes. Sure, some sequins in front, but in all honesty, they were topless! Smiling away!

Were my aunts pulling a joke on me? Or did they not know when they bought the tickets? Were they enjoying this? Is this typical for "adults?" I don't know, I'm not old enough to get into such places in the states. Would I want to?

Good Catholic girls are taught otherwise. Am I a prude? And I always obeyed my parents. But I start college in a few months. Am I an adult? Or when I turn eighteen in two months? Sure, I sneak and read my mom's Cosmopolitan magazines about sex. I glanced at more than a few Playboys in my dad's nightstand. I'll never look like those naked women.

But this is different. I didn't know how to act while watching a bunch of semi-nude ladies. I've never seen other women's bare breasts so close like this. I have two of my own! I just kept looking forward. Yes at, let me count…about twenty topless showgirls! Was the magician even doing magic tricks? I know he did complete at least one, when I saw that one lady on stage (with the largest breasts) was his assistant. Her back must hurt. These women wear these heavy, tall, headpieces. Why? Can anyone tell me what color any of these costumes are? Were we clapping over the magic trick or the women's bodies?

This twenty-something Arab's hand was still on my thigh. Great, he probably thinks this is normal for me. Watching topless women jiggle on stage. Maybe he was coming to this show and didn't plan on seeing me here. Why would he follow me?

So, I learned a few things during this hour plus of "adult entertainment."

First, I am not ready to be an adult and am now sexually confused. Second, my aunts are crazy for bringing me to this place. Did they enjoy this provocative entertainment? Personally, I was just in shock. But I had to pretend otherwise. It's not like when you leave a movie and comment to your friends about what you saw. What does one say after such an overexposure?

My aunts and I then parted ways, with no bare breast talk. They told me to be safe and meet up at five at the little boat to get to the ship. They didn't even notice the Arabian brothers in our row.

Nevertheless, the ladies were off to the casino for four hours.

*

I leave in a different direction from the casino. The door exits to a beach. I put my hat back on, now to sit and try and figure out what I just saw. The ladies onstage were great dancers, but what's my issue with nudity? As I step outside, I hear Zaran, "May I join you?" he asks ever so politely as he gets the door. Well, as I thought my day would not have included what I just witnessed, and I thought I wanted to photograph the Bahamas, why not change these expectations even further. Zaran excuses himself for a moment to find out about our location.

He returns to say that there is a more private part of the beach just a way down and they have cabanas so I can stay in the shade. Darn, he is thoughtful! As we start to walk down the beach, I am thankful for all of the bikini tops I see. But as we get further down, to the "private section" with the cabanas, there are more topless women again. "I

43

thought the Bahamas didn't allow topless beaches?" Why did I ask him that? (And after what we just witnessed, I guess anything goes.)

"It's okay on the private section," as he pulls a cabana cover a little over halfway up and I take off my sundress and lay on the lounge in my bikini. "Do you want me to put some lotion on you?" asking ever so politely. I oblige and he begins lathering up my back. I pull my hair up. Top of my neck and then shoulders. Then I could feel a bikini top string get untied. My heart is racing. I barely know this man. I glance around, and realize that I can't be seen by too many people. No one has a camera either. Why am I afraid? Honestly, not too many people have seen my breasts. I guess they look okay. Nothing like the men's magazines my dad hides. I know this is not an issue in Europe, but we really aren't in Europe. We are in the Bahamas. Then the next string is released and my top falls down. But he still just sees my back as he rubs my skin. His hands feel so good on my skin.

"Okay, your back is done." Crap, now it's time to turn around. Deep breath. This is Catie. Catherine is no longer here today. Around I go.

I take the suntan lotion and put some on my hands. How do I do this and not look sexual? Funny, I'm with an Arabian man, so I guess he has either seen women totally covered except their eyes, or has a harem and I am nothing new to him.

Is this even legal for a seventeen-year-old? Wait, he thinks I'm twenty and have probably done the wet t-shirt contests at college spring breaks like other crazy Americans. I over-think everything. Here goes, lotion all over my front, including my breasts that have never seen the light of day. I think my nipples are getting hard as they perk up. More deep breaths. Hat back on. Zaran faces the ocean and so do I. He barely noticed my breasts. He wasn't staring or gawking.

I wish I could photograph the blue sea. It is so clear. I mention this blueness to Zaran. He says he will be right back. Not knowing where he is going, I look around. Still topless. Ugh, I can't

SHOELESS

believe I am doing this. I pull up my shoulder length, curly, red hair into my beach hat, adjust my sunglasses and decide Catie will do something crazy. All alone, I walk up to the edge of the water. As I do this, another couple walks by me. They didn't even notice me. This really isn't an issue. I breathe some more. I look at the beautiful blue water. Crystal clear! Then someone walks up next to me with snorkeling gear. It was Zaran's brother Mehmet. "My brother went to get more gear. Do you want to snorkel?" It just occurred to me that Mehmet was seeing me without a top on. I didn't flinch, but I think my face turned beet red.

As I smiled, Zaran walks up with more fins. "Do you boys have a t-shirt I can put on so I don't get a sunburn in the ocean?" Zaran walks up to the cabana and comes back with his white t-shirt. It sure smells sexy. I take off my hat and he places the shirt over me. Now that felt more sexual than just being topless. I throw the hat up to our things and put on my fins. We are in the ocean and it is so clear and beautiful. Mehmet jokes and says he'd give me

$10,000 if I caught a fish with my hands. Like that would ever happen! I think he just liked to watch me jump up in a wet t-shirt. I was no Jacqueline Bisset, that's for sure.

After I give up on the fish catching, I decide to get back in the shade. Mehmet collects our gear to return it. Then he was off to the casinos. Meanwhile, I am in a dripping wet t-shirt and decide to take the plunge and remove it. Who am I? This little act of taking a top off in public may seem like nothing to some or most women, but I don't feel like a woman. I don't think I am breaking any of the Ten Commandments.

"Okay beautiful, do you want a drink?" Zaran asks. I am really not myself now, drunk with the Bahamas breeze and too much sun. I get up, look to see that the bar is within my view, and ask him what he wants and I'll go up and get it. Yes, ladies and gentlemen, without my top. A big hat and sunglasses, but only bikini bottoms and my Kino sandals from a previous trip to Key West. I start to get my wallet and Zaran laughs and says, "Beautiful, you won't need money for two drinks if you go up like this." I still grab some cash just in case.

Confidently, I head up to the bar. I remember a conversation my Great Aunt Emma gave me last Christmas. It was about confidence and "someday having to use my sexuality in certain situations." She continued, "Us redheads," she called me her twin (no other family member had red hair), "know that we have a special power over men." Well, I think all women do in their own way. "Just be cautious when you use it. It may not happen for a long time, but trust me, you will know. And it has nothing to do with what size you wear. Develop your inner confidence and it will get you anywhere you want to go in this world." Was this what she meant? Well, there was no sign of my cruise cabin mates or his brother. Some people look at me, rather, looked at my chest, but whatever. Let me clarify, the women older than me didn't look too happy with me, as some tried to distract their men. I am starting to believe this could be natural, as all women have them.

SHOELESS

As I order our drinks with a smile, a voice behind me says, "Catherine? Catherine Wells?" Do I dare answer or pretend it's not me? It's the weirdest and scariest feeling when someone recognizes you out of the United States, and you just happen to be without a shirt.

I pick up my drinks without having to pay, say thank you, to which I got a funny "No, thank you!" from the older bartender, and try and cover my nipples with the drinks as I turn around.

"Yes, it's you Catherine. I spotted that carrot top." Geez, how childish. Can't someone come up with a sexier name for a redhead? It's Mr. C, my high school freshman English teacher from that Catholic High School I just graduated from less than a week ago. (He had a long Polish last name that no one could pronounce after you read it, so he was just "Mr. C.") I am so embarrassed! I push the drinks closer to me to make sure that I'm covered. These drinks are so cold! What is he thinking now? He is such a sweet, caring, nice, middle-aged teacher. I had been a National Honor Society student! "Hey, I saw

49

you walking up to the bar." He had a strange look on his face. Definitely not that polite and humble teacher from a few years ago. I felt my face turn beet red again. "Boy, you're all grown up! And how you grew! So different than when you wore that uniform. You always kept that skirt well below the knees." He sounded so different. He was looking at me. Well, a certain area of me. Am I going to get a lecture? How I hoped he couldn't see my nipples. He probably did as I was walking up. This is creepy.

"You girls are sure exposing yourselves! Just a few nights ago I saw your former classmate Diane dancing at a club in Ft. Lauderdale. And she had on less than you when she was done!" What the hell was I supposed to say? He was so different. Even in his language.

I don't know what came over me as I started to speak. So here goes. "Mr. C, are you here with your wife?" No, that came out wrong.

He took it the wrong way. "Nope, I'm here with the guys," gesturing to a bunch of middle-aged men. "Care to join us? I'd love to introduce you with that topless swimsuit!" Deep breath. Exhale. Repeat. He's trying to see my nipples, but they are still covered by me holding the cold drinks. Then the "new Catie" made her vocal entrance into the world. I am certain that he already got more than an eyeful as I walked up to the bar.

(Catherine would never say this, let alone say it aloud): "Paul, it is Paul, right Mr. C? Are you curious to see more of what's under these glasses?" I look down at my covered breasts then right into his eyes. A sly smile of a yes came over his face. Now I was about to give this teacher a lesson he wouldn't soon forget. "If you want to enjoy more of this view, put your hand on top of your head." (He did it immediately.) I don't know where my mind was, but I moved the drinks to expose the full bare view of both of my breasts to him. "Do you like what you see? (Paul nods.) "Do you want something more out of these two gems?" (Still speechless, he nods again). "Oh, like what? To touch them, caressing each, or kiss them?" Who is saying this? Who am I? "Or would you lick them, suck them, bite them, pinch

51

them, put them between your...?" I look down and see him obviously growing and getting excited in his swimsuit. (Boy, I have read too many issues of Cosmo). As I continue, all I see is Paul looking right at my exposed breasts. Don't ever tell me men don't know how to react to a topless female, talking dirty. "Eyes up here. I would appreciate you never mentioning our seeing a little too much of each other here. To your friends, colleagues or even your wife. Why?"

I did the unthinkable. I leaned forward and my breasts touched his upper body, as I could feel his hard-on too against my leg. I whispered into his ear, "Because I am still a minor, and this would be illegal. Do you want to keep your job? Along with your reputation?"

I backed away and poured the drinks on his bathing suit. "Looks like you needed something cold down there!" His hands left his head. "How was that for a proper English lesson?"

This could have been something out of a version of a dirty book. I turned around, walked back up to the bar, asked for two refills and walked back to my cabana. What just happened? Who am I?

*

After giving the drink to Zaran, he asked me something strange. "So, you didn't catch a fish for the $10,000 my brother offered you. You don't need money? Would you consider something else for the money?" I immediately grabbed my towel and covered up. Can this day get any more Twilight Zoned?

"Not that, but I do want you to keep someone else busy for about an hour." I stood up. "No sex involved. Really. None. Unless *you* want me for some pleasure," He said as he held my hand and we walked on the beach, "Just dance with an old friend. I found out that he is on this cruise, and I don't want him to know I have anything to do with it."

"Do what?" I inquire.

53

"Just dance with him, and then I will surprise him!" I didn't know what Zaran was up to, but I felt as though I couldn't say no. I agreed, as we held hands walking down the beach. Why not, I've been adventurous like never before in my life, as long as I can keep my clothes on. Funny to say that, as I walk topless past the perverted teacher and his friends. "He will approach you on the dance floor. His name is Guillermo."

I ask the obvious, "Why will he approach me?"

Zaran laughs. "He has a real thing for beautiful women. Don't mention me. When you see me, come up to me."

Okay, for $10,000. Sure. It's like I'll ever see that money for something so simple. These wealthy guys sure play weird games. Today has been a weird game. But I wasn't Catherine today. I was topless Catie.

*

I meet my cabinmates (the room is too small to call them suitemates) at the dock and we head back to the ship. No mention of the earlier entertainment they subjected me to, only the fact that they won big at the casinos. Seemed they spent the entire day there on a $500 budget and brought back a $500 winning. To me that's break even. They were so excited about their "success," they didn't ask me about my day. Thank goodness...what would I have said?

We had a late dinner seating again and then they go straight to the slot machines onboard. They joke that they will probably play all night until we dock in Miami. They are definitely hooked. I guess that means more free time for me. So, I get Tess's sexy dress on again and I look at my chest in the mirror. I spritz some of Tess's perfume on all over, and borrow a pair of her extra lacy panties. I wait until eleven to go dancing. Somehow the thought of my Matthew, my high school love, never crosses my mind at all today. I feel somewhat hypnotized by this new exotic man.

The disco is packed, loud, and has the distinct aura of sexual desires. I walk in there with a new sense of self confidence. My first dirty little secret of this good Catholic girl. I start with a drink at the bar. Start dancing with lots of people. Again, this is really different from the prom a few weeks ago. Back to the bar and I order another drink. I've never had alcohol in public before this cruise, let alone two drinks. Rum and Coke it is. As I wait for this drink, I feel a hand go inside of the back of my dress, heading south. I slowly pull the hand out and look to see that it's not Zaran.

"Hello, I'm Liam." This hot man, with a Spanish accent, had his hand on my ass. Literally.

I reply with a coy, "Most people introduce themselves first. Then stick their hand down a woman's panties."

He laughs. "Come, let's dance!" He takes me to the dance floor and did the dirtiest of dances with me. I had never seen people dance like this. Let alone me! (I remember Y-100 coming to our school to d-jay a dance and I won a contest: got the H2O

Hall and Oats Album. But we did not dance like this!). We got so close that I could feel his front was hard in his pants. Then he turned me around and he was rubbing my backside. I swear it was as close to sex with your clothes on as possible. This dress didn't help either. Sure, it was low cut in both the front and back, but if you turned me a certain way, I'm sure you could see what was inside of my top. But, boy, did I feel exhilarated!

Others were dancing this way too. After shaking my bootie for a while, I had another drink. This time it's water. Liam was a charmer. It was too loud for a full conversation. I think I have a thing for guys with accents. Or maybe just his dark skin. After a while, I looked up and saw Zaran at the entrance. He smiled and waved at me to join him. I excused myself from Liam and headed for the door.

Zaran took my hand, put his other hand on the upper inside of my dress and kissed me. When his hand went there, I should have slapped him but something was drawing me closer to him in a hypnotic way. Then he actually looked back at Liam, smiled at him, and waved goodbye.

He took me to his hallway and kissed me again. All tongue and rougher this time. Is this normal for older guys? I've only had teenage boyfriends. He opened his door and all I saw was a huge cabin, complete with a king-sized bed, with music playing on the boom box. What do I do?

SHOELESS

"Call Me Maybe"
-Carly Rae Jepsen, Call Me Maybe

A cell phone starts to ring in the black bag I brought to McDonald's. It's not mine. Maybe Chars? I picked it up and answered it.

"Hello, beautiful." My heart sank. I couldn't speak. In that deep sexy voice of his, he said, "I owe you some money."

I dropped the phone and it hung up. It was the mystery man from McDonald's. Thirty years older, but now no stranger to me.

Rushing inside, I didn't know what to do. I hadn't heard from him since the flowers he sent me for my real 18th/ pretend 21st birthday the summer

59

after the cruise. I won't redial his number. Wait, I can't, it said BLOCKED.

I stay busy for the next few hours then decide to go to Holy Thursday services after dinner. I eat dinner alone again. But for only two more days. Oh, how my head is spinning. My husband knows nothing about the "Catie Cruise." Yes, I told him I went on the cruise, back when we met in 1986. I just left the last days out of any conversations. In fact, no one on the planet knows of these days. I killed "Catie" as I left the ship and came back to being just "Catherine" or now "Cat" to my family and friends. Should I go to confession before church tonight? Well, I don't think it's offered tonight, as it is Holy Thursday. As I check the bulletin for details, I ponder how ridiculous that confession would sound. Since Matt and I have been parishioners for twenty-five years there, and we had our kids' sacraments there, and the priests consider us "good and giving people" of our Time, Talent and Treasure, I think they'd think Mrs. Catherine Garcia has gone crazy. Throughout the years with Matt, I would occasionally say "I'm sorry," just out of the blue. Mostly in our bed, as we snuggle. How I've wanted to tell him, I just never did. How would I begin? He would think I was a slut. I have been ever so honest and true to him for our entire married life. Basically, except for this and a couple of other situations. I wonder if he knew about "Catie," would he still have wanted me to marry me? But this did happen before I even met him. We have been so happy and in love for over 25 years. Did I start our life together with this lie of not telling him everything?

Before I leave for church, I hear the jingle on the radio saying, "Hoops, there it is!" I try calling again for G-105's Hoops Match Game. I didn't get through the line. These people calling in the past few days are certainly not paying much attention, or even listening, because their numbers to match are pure guesses. Come on people, we are in the home stretch, as most of the numbers have been called. I promise, if I win the Butterball Turkey Deep Fryer, I'll give it to my favorite guy on the radio, Bob of

"Bob and The Showgram." I have an addiction to winning on the radio, or at least trying.

As I enter the church, I get a nervous feeling. Like my almost perfect life is about to explode. I look around the church. Is Zaran here? I can't concentrate, let alone pray. Oh, how I look around and see those young, female, teenage lectors and choir singers wearing their skirts or dresses ever so short. We are at church, not a nightclub. If they bend over, the priest will certainly get a view. But I forgot, they too are just men. Trust me: they will never implement a "decency clause" on what to wear at the altar. Why am I like this? Remembering all of my two slutty days in my life is doing something to my mind. I go back home to a dark house. Zaran's cell phone rings again.

"Catie, we need to talk." It's that unique sort of Spanish and Saudi accent. My ADHD mind is going a million miles an hour.

"How did you find me? And why now, after all of these years?"

"Facebook .and YouTube. You're quite the little saver." He was right about being a saver. I started couponing for "Free," "Nearly Free," and "Money Makers," a little over a year ago. I thought, heck, if I can do it, anybody can. So, I started my own YouTube Channel (without paid commercials) to teach others how to do it. I look at it as my special ministry to those in need. Or anybody. I saved over $3000 in personal and household products so far in less than a year and a half. I give a lot away and have a stockpile that should last my family for about a year. I tell everyone to join and follow oh, what's his name, that Dude, my favorite Extreme Couponer, to learn more and make couponing friends throughout the country.

"Why the secrecy in McDonald's today?" I ask. "Why are you here?"

"I still have the money I owed you from years ago. And I tracked you down to finally give it to you."

I was perplexed. "What are you talking about?"

"The $10,000 from the cruise. You never collected it." I didn't collect it because I was still underage at the time when he sent me flowers for my 18th, he thought 21st birthday, and the note on the card said to meet him at The Bounty to collect my gifts. "When you didn't show up, I thought you didn't want to see me again. I have thought about you often throughout these years Catie." Oh, that pronunciation of my name gives me chills. Except for the cruise, I was never, nor did I want to, be called Catie, with or without his accent, again. He continues, "Then, through the power of the internet, we magically meet again!" Back in 1985, communication was limited to landline telephones and snail mail.

Was he serious about giving me the money? That would certainly help with my old business IRS bill. But what exactly did I do almost 30 years ago for the $10,000?

"Go to your back door." Oh Lord was I scared, is he here? I'm alone, but somehow, I think he knows that. I turn the back-porch light on. I open the door, look out the screen door and see a small box. As I look around the backyard, there is nobody outside.

"Catie, as you open it, you will find a little extra." I go back inside and lock the doors. I start to count the hundred-dollar bills, but am so confused.

"Zaran, what do you want from me?" I lay on the couch. He begins, "I saw on the web that you are a photographer."

I quickly interrupt, "I used to be, until the industry changed a few years ago."

"But you still know your art, right?"

I then answer, "Of course, why?"

He continues: "If my memory serves me correctly, you wanted to be in the fashion end of photography. I saw your images on Google. Well, I have a client that is looking for a photographer, at a day rate, currently $10,000, to photograph some up and coming models in New York City. Would you be interested?"

"Seriously, why me? I do something else now." This is surreal. I add, "I am also married." I don't know why I said this. I am so confused.

"Be that as it may, you made that clear at lunch," he chuckles. "I just located you on Facebook and the memories came flooding back. Do you remember?" Oh do I. There's something about this man that stops everything in your life. Is this happening again? Does he want me or just my talents, as a photographer?

"Yes, I remember all of it." I take a deep breath. "A client? What do you do now?"

Zaran goes on to explain that he became an international attorney. (As we discussed on the cruise.) His client is in advertising.

I want to know more, since this is the dream job I had always wanted. "When is this photo shoot?"

"It's on Memorial Day. Can you fit it in your schedule?"

SHOELESS

The first thing that comes to mind is that it's on a holiday, so I will have the day off. But what do I tell my husband? "I'm not sure. I'll have to get back to you on that. What number can I call you at?" He tells me that he will call me again in a month from tonight. There's a phone recharger at the bottom of the box filled with money. This is weird, so surreal. Is this really happening? I put the phone in my nightstand, along with a shoebox containing $20,000. It's now in a hidden compartment at the bottom drawer. It's next to other "treasures" of mine, including the only complete journal I ever wrote. From 1985. It's missing two days in May.

He must have some great mutual funds to collect that kind of interest! What can a person do with that kind of cash? It will red flag any bank as a cash deposit.

I turn on the evening news. A landslide just happens to occur today on the private island off Washington state that I am supposed to visit in July with my nanny family. Wow! The great thing about

SHOELESS

this new job is that I travel a lot with them, so this will definitely be an adventure.

SHOELESS

"I Want You to Stay"
-Rihanna, Stay

The month goes by rather quickly. Matt returns only to tell me that he will be going back to Mexico every month for the next few months in two week stretches. They are trying to set up a clinic there. I figure it's better than "Doctors without Borders" for us, because that is almost a year commitment, plus the fact that they are currently not seeking PA applicants. I don't stop him with his passion, nor does he mine. But somehow, I don't mention New York City to him. He will be away. Plus, it's only for a day. This is the first time in our married life that I am deceiving him. (No. I just lied.) I debit extra cash out when I go to Wal-Mart to get groceries. He never sees the receipts. While I'm there at the store, I stop by and carefully look at each of the Missing and Exploited Children they have posted either at their entrance or Customer Service Department. Each is somebody's child. My heart breaks for them and their families. I wish I could help them.

Oh, after we filed our 2012 taxes, a nice DO IT NOW action letter came from the IRS. Apparently, they found out on our last return a few weeks ago that I am gainfully employed again and want their money. I have thirty days to respond. I have all of this money, yes, in a shoebox, but can't really give it to them. At least in a huge chunk! I decline to mention the shoebox to Matt. I am starting to feel like Catie again. What would God say?   What am I doing?

I went back to work to my nanny family. These boys say the cutest things. I told the three-year old that he definitely has his mom's genes, as they look identical. As he looks down at his pants, he says, "No Miss Cathy, these are *my* jeans!"

The news about the Boston Marathon Bombers that are brothers is all over the news. I keep thinking about Zaran and his brother. At least they are not involved in crime. Or are they? I don't know anything about them. I research Facebook. Yes, "research," not "creeping." Nothing. Google: nothing. Guess that's good news. So how did he see me on Facebook? I have my privacy settings on Friends Only.

Zaran called back, on that certain day, and after careful consideration, (it was all I'd thought about), I said yes. I figure Matt will be in Mexico, and I can have my dream job for a day! I ask about his brother, Mehmet, to which he grimly responded that he died a few years ago. He has no family left.

Also, in the world news was the rescue of the Cleveland Kidnapper. Three adults and one child found in a house. How can such crime happen in a little neighborhood house? And no one knew for so many years?

Surprise! We didn't win the Powerball on May 18! I tried for the first time in years. That would have been any easy excuse for one payment to the IRS. I finally called the IRS and after being on hold forever, set up a payment arrangement from now until eternity. I guess I can send them as certified checks using the cash. Just another secret from my husband. I've never been this kind of person. Our marriage and I used to be different. No, it's all my fault.

Some good news: I did win the iHEART RADIO Ultimate Pool Party Contest! I texted those special words every hour for weeks and got two tickets and the works! Matt will be in Mexico, so I asked Char. A girls' weekend in Miami. It's not until the end of June, but it is something else to look forward to! I haven't shared any of the Zaran story, even though she talked with him in McDonald's and had no idea of who he was.

The Sunday before Memorial Day, Matt and I go to Assaggio's, our favorite Italian restaurant down by Millbrook and Glenwood Avenue. It's really the best Italian food in Raleigh. Everything seems to be fine until I ask him about his upcoming trip. He tells me the names of the participants and I don't know any of them, so I ask if they were the same people as last time. I get an explanation of how some people can't get off as much as he can. I immediately chime in with "Can't get off work? You're doing this without pay. How can you get off so much?" All I saw was the IRS bill lurking. He says I'm in charge of paying that bill off. Oh, I started a fight. I didn't mean to fight. We hardly ever fight. But it's usually about money, or our lack of having money. I know he makes more money than me, and my old business debt is my own. Still. I wouldn't have that debt since I chose to pay us instead of them when the business started failing.

We finished lunch in silence and drove to the airport in dead silence. I hate this kind of argument. I can't remember the last time we argued this way. I want him to stay so we can talk this out. I am confused. This time I just dropped him off at the curb, and I watched him go through the sliding glass doors. He doesn't even look back at me. I see a young woman with extra-long brown hair run up to him and give him a hug. I don't think twice about this, because, seriously, what am I about to do?

Maybe it's just business. But I do remember what I'm up to in New York. Stop. I will be faithful. Keep telling myself that. I'm over thinking again. All this man wants is my photographic talents. So, I spend the rest of the day at Barnes and Noble scouring fashion magazines for the latest trends.

My "special" phone rings and Zaran confirms tomorrow's elaborate plans. I forget that I saw my husband leave, well, get on a plane with, another woman. How hypocritical would that be? How I wanted to talk with Matt, but I know that we have an arrangement to have him call me on Sundays when he is not with me. Usually Skype. If he's in the city he gets better cell reception and will call. Then we can see each other. But we left on not-so-great terms. Today was Sunday, and no call. Did I really want him to call?

SHOELESS

"I see the future, but live for the moment,"
-Pitbull featuring Christina Aguilera,
Feel This Moment

I'm back at RDU airport on Monday morning, Memorial Day, and secretly fly to NYC. My time is my own today, as the kids don't check in from college with their "adult" lives too often. Plus, I have the day off of work. I packed some of my cash just in case I needed something. Except for going down the three-story indoor waterslide at a work vacation, I can't remember the last time I felt so exhilarated. I was greeted off of the plane by Zaran, with a great smile. Met by a man other than my husband. This is so wrong. This is the first time that I have seen him since McDonald's a few

75

months ago. "Catie," still pronounced "caught-ee," still sends chills all around me as Zaran hugs me, and kisses my cheek. He still smells gorgeous, just like all of those years ago. He is extremely muscular. And so nicely dressed in a suit that I know was not from Target.

Oh, God, what am I doing? "The car is outside, come." I only have a backpack, so we don't have to wait for any luggage. A car, this was not! It was a black limousine. I haven't been in one since my wedding day! What is he expecting from me? Am I really doing this? Doing what? I try to justify this as a way to earn a lot of money legally to pay back my taxes. Plus, this one day in my life doing my dream job: being a fashion photographer in New York City!

I've never been to New York City. It is loud, crowded, has a certain stench (a cross of car pollution and well, garbage in spots). "We must go straight to the studio. All of the equipment is ready for you," Zaran begins. "Nikon, right?" Funny, but seriously, only professionals would know that if you're a Nikon girl, you can't do Canon. It's been over two years since I have picked up any camera other than my phone. I say a quick prayer. That was probably a mistake. I'll be shot to hell for even being here. What am I doing? This faithful, Catholic, middle-aged lady, is lying to herself. But he only wants me for my photographic skills, right?

"Yes sir," I smirk.

"Catie, you will be meeting with William Gonzalez, the owner of this venture. You can "Yes, Sir" him all you want. Be that as it may, you may not 'Sir' me. You are the same Catie from the cruise? Right?" I smile. He continues, "Capeesh?" That word sounds funny in his Saudi accent.

"Capeesh" I return. "What have you been up to all of these years?" Just curious, since I am in a limousine with a hunk, even after all of these years, whom I really don't know. Did once, really well, but really didn't know who he was to the world.

"We can, how do you say it, chit chat and catch up after your session. You have a full day. I

77

can't stay long, but will pick you up later for your flight. Did you bring the phone?" I took it out my bag and handed it to him. He touched my hand. I still get goose bumps at his touch. Then he switches out the SIM card on the phone. "My number is the only one under contacts, should the need arrive."

This is weird. I respond with a "Thanks, are you married?"

"My Catie, why should this matter? We will dialogue later."

Seriously? Why did I ask him that? He obviously doesn't want me that way. Sexually. I shouldn't even be thinking like this. I am married! Even though we fought, I am still madly in love with my husband. Where is my head? New York City of course, as Zaran points out various places. We drive over the Brooklyn Bridge. It is even more magnificent than the PBS documentary I viewed a few months ago. Did I just see a woman rollerblading topless on the Brooklyn Bridge? Where is my mind? Of course not. No, I really did see a topless rollerblader. I think this is first time I've seen another woman topless (other than the movies) since I was with this man so many years ago. I wonder if he sees my facial expression. The limo turns off of the bridge and we arrive at a huge warehouse type of building.

Zaran helps me out of the limo and lets go of my hand. Yup, nothing. Good. Down to business.

As I enter this warehouse, it is everything I expected. The highest of ceilings, dressing rooms, and loud music. A man about late fifties or early sixties walks over, shakes my hand and introduces himself as William Gonzalez, complete with a Hispanic accent. And he calls me darling! Just the way Pitbull pronounces it, *Dah-r-lyn.* After explaining what he wants, that would be twenty females photographed, looking attractively sexy, in a couple of outfits, like for composites and later for their Book.

I am ready. I head over to my "team:" the makeup artists, clothing stylists, lighting crew and digital production advisors, and introduce myself. Everyone is really nice.

The whole day happened so quickly. In eight hours, I photographed twenty teenage girls, in about three outfits each, close up and full length, and had time for a quick sandwich and two bathroom breaks. There wasn't time to chat with any of the models, let alone any of the crew. We finished up about five o'clock and Mr. Gonzalez was happy with the results. I know Zaran was back and had been standing in the corner at one of the monitors, smiling.

As both men went to the other part of the room to chat, I go over to another monitor to see my work. I slip in a flash drive connected to my keychain to save my images so I can critique my work later, in case I get this assignment again. I know I shouldn't be "stealing" these, but I want to think more about poses for next time. (Presuming there is a next time.) No one sees me do this, so what harm can it do?

The men walk over to me and Zaran puts his arm around my shoulder, stating, "I knew Catie was the one for this assignment. Good job. We must leave to catch your flight." I hold out my hand to Mr. Gonzalez, thank him and tell him I would look forward to any future endeavors.

My flight wasn't until eight, thank goodness, because we just about got over the Brooklyn Bridge when the driver told us they were closing the bridge because of some car left on the side of the bridge. Terrorist act? I don't know. I'll see it on the news later back in Raleigh.

"You did a good job, Catie. Would you like to do this type of work again?" Zaran asked, but it sounded like a statement. In reality, I would like to return. But is this reality?

"Is this for real?" I just had to ask. Yes, I knew I did the job, but I hadn't seen a paycheck, let alone fill out any tax forms. "If it is, I won't be available until the end of July, that's when I get six weeks off of work for summer vacation."

"Be that as it may," he begins, "Your next trip to the Big Apple must be for more than one day. I am sure William would want you for more extended projects. Let me talk with him to confirm some dates and I will make all of the arrangements. Before I exit the limo, Zaran leans over and kisses my cheek. "No, I have never married," followed by, "Your compensation for today's services will be on your back porch again." Wow! Did he say stay overnight next time? Crap, more cash?

As I fly back to RDU, my seatmate is reading that "mommy porn book." Yes, this "good little Catholic girl" has read it. What I don't understand is why can't there be a hot book about people over, or way over the age of forty? Those characters are in their twenties. Honestly, I think sex got much better after forty! And that S&M, what my generation called it before they added more letters to that stuff, really isn't all that necessary. Sure, try a few, and enjoy. But fisting, as it was mentioned on "The List," seriously? (I had to Google this word's definition.) I had four little ones come out of me there, and yes, I feel pretty "tight" again, but who wants an entire fist full of knuckles up you twisting about? I don't see having a bruise like black-and-blue mark inside of you for days as any bit enjoyable. Way off topic, again. Sorry, I'm a professional "ADHD-er."

SHOELESS

"I'm gonna pop some tags..."
-Macklemore & Ryan Lewis
featuring Wanz, <u>Thrift Shop</u>

So much to do and so little time! I don't hear from Zaran, remembering him telling me he had business to do out of the country.

I get back into work the next day, about fifty hours per week, and look forward to my long, six-week paid vacation as my "Nanny Family" travels in Europe. Summertime nannying includes daily trips to "The Club," where I bring all four boys to the pool. It's a different world for me, for as soon as I tell the front desk the last name of the family I care for, a mimosa is automatically brought to me at the table by the pool. Seriously? Yes, I could be in the age range of the mother, but it's just funny. I can't ever drink it though, as I still have two little boys that don't know how to swim and that need my full attention while in the pool.

The big news at work to share is that as I'm at the family's house getting the boys changed after swimming, I hear this wicked gushing sound. As I run to the playroom, I see water spouting everywhere from the oversized fish tank! The two older boys were throwing a football around and it crashed into the fish tank and cracked it! Just another day nannying four busy boys. Luckily, the boys and I "saved" about a dozen of the several dozen existing pets and put them in the bathtub. The parents seemed okay about the situation and called the "Fish Guys" to come over and clean up the mess and replace the tank. Wow, in "my world" I would have had to clean it up, probably flush the fish and say enough of fish! These "fish guys" had a new aquarium up and running with filters and fancy coral within a few hours of calling them. Oh, the world of having a lot of money. I'll never see it. Or will I now?

Off to "Storytime" we go. This day is actually more exciting than usual, as we nannies notice a hot daddy with his toddler across the room. He looks familiar. Oh, how I don't like it when I don't recognize someone immediately. Aha! I Google a name on my iPhone and show the other nannies. It's that cute news anchor from the local news! Well, then the other nannies start taking pictures of him across the room. Man, we need a new adventure. Wait, my "other life" is certainly an adventure!

Matt comes home from Mexico and we talk it out. We are fine. I know that he is a giving, caring, loving, and honest person. I, on the other hand, am not. Period. Exclamation point! I have not told him about my trip to New York City. He leaves again for Mexico every two weeks on, two off. I don't badger about details anymore. He says and acts like he still loves me. I do too. Our lovemaking seems different. Not in a good way, nor a bad way. Is it me? My guilt of impure thoughts of wanting to be with another man? I'm torn between Matt and Zaran.

Work has me travelling again. This time to Kiawah Island, South Carolina. Gorgeous is an understatement. All I can say is that I rode a bicycle for the first time since grade school, and for twelve miles the first day! My legs could feel it. This was with all four little ones too! On the pavement and along the beach. We were so close to alligators in the water near us on the sidewalk. My blood pressure was sky high! What a workout! We did go to another exclusive club on the beach that had a pool. A Sunday brunch to die for! I have never seen shrimp so big! And I'm still losing weight! See, I am just a normal hard worker, just happen to have a lot of extra money hanging around in a shoebox. However, I am a little nervous because I am getting a lot of sun. I'm awfully tired after each fun day in the sun. I am reapplying sunscreen almost every twenty minutes. Excessive, yes. However, there is not much shade here and I can't afford a massive sunburn.

SHOELESS

The next day, we bike on the sand to the golf club. Wow! This place reminds me of Boca Raton while growing up (except for biking on the sand). Opulence is everywhere here. I must look like a country hick wearing my Target clothes and big hat. (Don't get me wrong, I LOVE Target, it's just that I don't think this family has ever been inside of one. You get the picture.) The family I help is ever so nice, mind you, I just feel so out of place. I hope I don't embarrass them as the kids eat their $12, a piece, peanut butter and jelly sandwiches.

SHOELESS

"Cause you're amazing just the way you are..."
-Bruno Mars, Just the Way You Are

I get Friday off, which is perfect because Char and I are heading to Miami for the iHeart Music Festival that I won. Plane tickets to Miami and two nights at the Fontainebleau Hotel on Miami Beach. After over twenty years of friendship this is our first girls' weekend get-a-way! We were either too busy with the kids growing up or was a monetary issue. This is basically free since I won it on G-105. However, I packed some of those $100 bills from my 1985 "job" to really have fun! No dollar menu items for us this weekend. We deserve a special trip!

The one thing that I can say about our special friendship is that we always tell each other the truth, but I can't reveal my trip, Zaran, or my past on the cruise to her, my best friend. I feel like a fraud. I do hope she has fun though. I say that because she has different musical and religious ideas. She's a conservative, very conservative Catholic and I am just a Catholic.

I'm still trying to actually understand that term for myself. I was raised Catholic, and still go to church each week, but I don't believe or follow some of their teachings. I don't read the Bible or can even quote much from it, where Char is on day 29 online (I'm following her progress on Facebook!). I'm still trying to find God, and all the other stuff that is preached. I do find myself listening more in depth to our priests' homilies, but then again, they are single men. On the plane down to Miami, we discuss our new Pope. Char doesn't seem too thrilled with him, since he seems like such a different person than the Pope we just had in the Vatican. Maybe this man will change things for the Catholic Church. Lord knows that we need it. Heck, I even joke with her that he could be Time Magazines Man of the Year! (I know, that will never happen.)

We enter the Fontainebleau, and see The Staircase! We see it all and it is magnificent! We check in, get our passes and wrist bands and decide to first go up to our room. People are so nice here. The outdoor festivities have begun. In summary, I can say that of all the singers and bands that the lead for Iconna Pop's hair is really red, like flaming red! Jason Derulo was hot without his shirt, "YES, I'M MARRIED, NOT DEAD," as he jumps in the pool, (that boy can dance!), Krewella has too many tattoos, and Jason, again, can do a mean handstand (then tearing another shirt off!). We saw most of this from afar, as one, I wanted shade, and two, since there were cameras taping, I thought it best that my body in a swimsuit stay clear of that production. I was saving America by not showing this body on camera! (Even though I've lost over twenty pounds this calendar year walking the baby around the neighborhood plus Weight Watchers!)

On the second morning, Char and I decide to head toward the beach. No nightlife for us! Fully sun screened and large hats, towels and bags, we looked like a couple of tourists from the north. But as we got closer to the sand, I realized we were NOT like everyone else! Char declares, "Run the other way!" which is kind of funny coming from a woman that uses a crutch to help her walk. I look around. This is not the same Miami Beach as when I went to college. It reminded me of the Bahama beach many years ago. But I'll never tell her that I went topless, when "the girls" were perkier. Now with the advent of the iPhone, Twitter, Instagram, Facebook, YouTube, etc., I will not take them out in public. It would mortify my adult children! Yes, South Beach is top optional. Really?

"Charlotte, we're here for fun. Now come with me. Trust me, for the sake of the world, we are keeping our tops on! We both have two of them, like these ladies here, only mine droop a bit more, especially out of these suits with the pushups enclosed!"

We laugh and drag our supplies closer to the water. The same as almost thirty years ago, everyone's are a little different, and no one really says anything about it.

I still have issues. Is it me, or are young people just not modest? Toplessness seems to be everywhere in today's culture. From reality shows to the internet, it seems like no big deal to them. Was this the first time in thirty years I've seen other women topless? Well, not belonging to a gym, going in saunas or anything else where this would be an issue...oh wait, I really think I saw a woman on the Brooklyn Bridge rollerblading without a shirt. (I should Google that!) Yes, I did my crazy Catie days, but Cat is here now. Not happening!

We end up in the ocean having fun in the waves, trying not to get knocked down. During the last few years, since being hit by a texting driver, Char has always had the philosophy that yes, something bad has happened to her and she walks with crutches, but it didn't stop her life. So here we are, jumping the waves! One however, was too strong, and knocked her under. She got back up coughing fiercely, and I started to drag her back to shore. Two bare-breasted women came bouncing down to the water's edge and asked us if we needed help. Way too funny, we both crack up hysterically.

As we head back to the elevator, Char seems to have dropped her towel somewhere in the sand. I tell her that I will go back, and she can just head on up. Her one crutch was really full of sand, and I knew she had a hard time on the beach with that. (This one is so different from the sand in Kiawah, which was solid and firm enough to bicycle ride to the golf club on it!).

I was back at Boobville and found the towel. I don't think I have the issues about taking my top off as I did it long ago. I could actually do it at this moment. But with technology today, I could see my face and droopy breasts would have headlines splattered across the internet with the words "Mature" in the title. At least there were no cameras or cell phones when I did it long ago.

SHOELESS

As I walk towards the elevator, I see a man that looks like William from the NYC photo shoot. He is with several other men, and a skinny bitch type with long shiny black hair. They are in deep conversation. I decide to get on the elevator as quickly as possible, to avoid them. What would I say to Char if he saw me?

As I went back up the elevator, I decided to nap, as the sun exposure really did me in. I was severely sick a few years ago and tested positive for lupus and the docs basically told me to stay out of the sun. (I thought it meant not to get a sunburn, but I get so tired in sunshine that I think they mean to stay out of the sun in general. I will look it up on the internet.) We, meaning the doctors and I, would "deal with this disease after something else occurs." So far nothing, but I try and rest a lot. This was a week of sun! First, Kiawah sunshine and the pools and beaches, and now this. As I rest, Char goes back to reading her Bible. I wish I had such faith. Or is it religion? Whichever, I lack it.

I hear Char crying. And I turn around to see her on her bed. "Cat, can we talk? I mean really talk?" I sit up and hand her a tissue.

"What is it?"

"All of those breasts we just saw."

"Okay," I wonder, where is she going with this?

"I wish I was better endowed like you," she states and I start to giggle.

"What? These are a pain in the ass. I can't find a supportive bra that doesn't give me shoulder and back pain. I can't go without a bra or I look like trailer trash, and I would like to have a conversation with a man that has his eyes up here and not there." I pause and continue my boob monologue. "Plus, they look a hell-of-a-lot better with a bra or pretty soon I will be looking like one of those African women in National Geographic magazines." She laughs, and I continue. "Okay, they don't droop that much. I don't think! Where is this coming from?

You've always seemed to be such a self-confident, beautiful, I'll wear my own style, kind of dame!"

She sniffles. "I came home from work early one day and I saw Rob on one of our son's bed looking at a laptop. He said he was borrowing our son's computer and he saw these topless women on our sons' history. I don't know how long he was looking, or what he found, and we never really finished the conversation except for the fact that he would have a talk with our son."

"Well, okay. Did he talk with him?" I wonder what one would say to a single 25-year-old man.

"It's not that, our son came home to dinner, you know, he still lives with us!" I chuckle. She cries harder. "I saw he had his laptop in his backpack, the one upstairs wasn't his," I got it and gave her a hug. "Cat, we haven't talked about it for weeks now. What is it about breasts and men? Oh, your husband's in the medical profession, so he must have a different view…"

"Wait, stop, I'm sick of hearing from Matt that *the body is a beautiful thing*. It would be if he called me beautiful every once and a while. Do you remember that guy at McDonald's we saw months ago? When he called me beautiful? That was the first time I heard that word in forever. Yes, I hear, *you look nice, pretty*, whatever. But "beautiful" is such a strong word for me! Honestly, I wouldn't feel comfortable if Matt was here with us and had been on the beach with us earlier. First, I always have to have my clothes on in the daytime, in our own house! I thought it would be different once the kids left! I came downstairs topless once and he ran to close the shades! He was worried about both the neighbors and Google Earth snapping our house photo at that minute!" She laughs, I keep talking, "Seriously, that's what he said. It's not like I went out on the back porch. God forbid! And we didn't even have sex after this. I thought it would spark an interest. Nope. Medical professional or not, he's still just an American male. The media has screwed us all up. They want the retouched young thing, while we feel inadequate small or large, as large usually means stretch marks if they are natural."

Char continues my thought, "You're right. As Catholics we are taught that sex is for procreation. But is nudity sacred or profane? An act between a husband and wife, or a desired pleasure just amongst two people?" Oh, she threw in Catholicism. "Cat, see, even I relate breasts to sex. I wish I didn't have the hidden dangers I found in my marriage. Yours is so stable."

I wish I could tell her the truth. Not just about our McDonald's mystery man, but my past, and even my present. I am just starting to realize that Matt gets texts at all hours, has locked his phone and laptop with passcodes, which he has refused, yes, refused, to share. Oh, my world is full of secrets. Not just from me, but could he be hiding some too? Here I go, over thinking again.

I announce, "Well, let's cover up and look sexy tonight! I still think covering some flesh can be hotter than baring it all. It's the mystery! It's all in the mind! Let's go have some more fun!"

SHOELESS

After dinner, we head to the night performances. Enrique Iglesias introduces Pitbull! WOW! Both of them onstage, I'm in heaven. As I jump up and down and sing along, Char gives me a crazy look. (She's more a country music and not Top 40 kind of lady!) He closes saying, "Pleasure to be with you in your crib Miami, as Mr. 305, Worldwide: check-n-out, God Bless, DAHLYN!" Oh my God!

SHOELESS

"You helped me see the beauty in everything..."
-Kelly Clarkson, Catch My Breath

As I fly into RDU from Miami, Matt flies in from Mexico! We have two days together until I leave with my nanny family to go to Seattle and the private island off of Washington. Matt is ecstatic about the progress being made on the medical clinic in Mexico.

He isn't too happy about us being apart on the Fourth of July. "Cat, we've had every holiday together until now. It's one of your favorites: fireworks, the State Fairgrounds."

I quickly interrupt, "No, remember, they moved the Raleigh fireworks downtown last year, and all we saw were the buildings downtown." Not the excuse he wanted.

"But we can go to Brier Creek," he chimed in.

"Hon, I know that we are going to be apart, again, but this job is important to me. They are counting on me. Plus, we need the money so I can pay the IRS bill." I am quite a reliable employee, having been late only once due to traffic problems on I-40. However, this trip is for eight days.

I start to cough. "Sweets, are you okay?" he says. The coughing continues. I dig into my backpack for my inhaler. Weird, I even needed it this past weekend in Miami, and the air there seems so different. Maybe I'm catching a cold. But I feel kidney stones coming on again too! What is my body doing? "If you don't rest, you'll be no good to that family."

We get home and I spend the next few days in bed. Still coughing. Matt is helping me as much as possible, but I sleep a lot. I was so ill that we weren't even able to make love while he was home. I miss our special time together. Our schedules will overlap now. I am gone for eight days, and he leaves two days before I return.

The Nanny Family and I travel all the way to the West Coast. My first time ever! It took two flights. Planes are an adventure for these four little ones. Except for the baby, who is in a stroller, each of these kids has their own little rolling suitcase. As we walk through the corridors, they line up in back of each other, little blonde ducklings. Too cute! Thank goodness these planes have televisions at each seat.

Upon our arrival, the parents go to get us a car to get to the hotel. It was a limousine! Everyone was so excited. They asked me if I had ever been in a limo, and I said yes, at my wedding many years ago. I could not mention the fact that I was just in one in New York City. They (well no one) knows that I even went there!

We start off at the Sheraton in Seattle. Simply gorgeous suite. The adults will go and do whatever they do, and I will have the kids. It was neat in that they gave me the mornings off, after breakfast, so they could be a family and I could have my free time. (I'm not a live-in back home, but had fourteen-hour days in Seattle as they stayed out late and the baby was up at five).

Since I have never been anywhere alone, except shopping back home, I was skeptical on where to visit. So, I went to the concierge and asked where the nearest Catholic church was located. (Downtown Seattle is full of all the fancy stores we have back home, and I wanted something different.) She showed me a map and handed me a preprinted directional guide on how to get there. Should take about fifteen to twenty minutes on foot. My sneakers were laced up and I was ready to go! I have never been hiking before, let alone walk in an unknown city, but I felt brave. This is not normal for me.

I get to the area in the directions that is a shortcut through the freeway or take a left and go over it. I choose the latter. Wow, I can see the cars below! New experience. Then I cross a street at what seems to be close to the cathedral and I get to walk past a large white Cadillac complete with loud music, and an African American man wearing a huge white hat. Seriously! He is stopped and I decide to put my head up tall, walk firmly, and make eye contact but nothing else. The cathedral is across the street, I go up the steps and photograph the outside.

I did it! Trust me, this may not seem like an adventure to some, but I've lived a rather quiet, easy, probably boring life, to some. I worried too much, but I am determined to change. It's a beautiful place, and I even picked up a little soft cover book of the Living Faith Catholic Devotions that I found in a pew. I'm still full of religious questions, and need to start somewhere. I stick the booklet in my back pocket. After looking at the time, I venture back to the hotel and stop across the street to buy some soup. My throat is really bothering me. The kids and I play, and go to the pool. The sun doesn't set until after nine, so my fourth of July fireworks outing was a bust. The parents went out, and I got to see the fireworks from a distance 26 floors up. I miss my husband.

The next day their cousins come down from their home in Whidbey Island, where we will be in a few days. They take the older boys back with them and all I have are the younger boys for a few days! We venture to the park and back to the pool. I did go to Walgreens on my morning off and picked up a few bottles of Gatorade to help my throat. I gave one of the bottles, along with one of my protein bars to a homeless young man on the street corner. There are so many homeless people here in this area in Seattle.

The five of us pack up and head to the island to visit more of their family. They rented a minivan and I must say, the people in Seattle are such polite drivers. There is no honking! We go on a ferry, and the mom and I get out to walk around. It was quite chilly. I take some photographs of the scenery on my phone. This family has taken me to some beautiful places. The mountains remind me of something you would see in a National Geographic magazine. As we arrive, the house in on a cliff! They assured me that the landslide earlier this year was on the other end of the island. As I look out of their backyard, all I see is the Pacific Ocean and the most beautiful view of the Olympic Mountains. It's breathtaking.

The only "bad side," if one can call it that, is that this family has cats. Lots of them. My room had probably been where the cats played and slept, because I start wheezing and sneezing. I pop an allergy pill to help. I think I'm too late. Inhaler time. So, this new adventure begins!

We go visit a state park. That's an understatement. We hike through this park. Remember that just the other day I "hiked" to the Cathedral, well, this is a real "hike" in nature. Another first for me. But my allergies are killing me, plus that lingering cough.

At this part of the trip, my afternoons are mine. So, I rest! I turned on my phone once and caught up on answering comments from my YouTube Couponing Followers. I still try to put something out each week, but I've been ever so busy. I did view some Facebook posts, and noticed a missing girl alert. Either kids are starting to look alike, or she had something familiar about her. Where have I seen her? It was just her basic school photo, but it was a weird feeling. She's only twelve and has been missing for a little over a month. If I was that girl's mom, I'd be out of myself with worry! I click "share" and hope my friends will pass this along. My coughing continues.

The next day I dare myself to do something even more adventurous than the trek to the Cathedral and the State Park hike! I will "go down the cliff" to reach the ocean. Since this house is literally on a cliff, they have about three hundred homemade stairs, in various shapes, sizes and materials, from the top by the house, to the bottom at the beach. I take it slow, and say several prayers. I am so nervous! You have to be careful not to have a certain plant touch your skin or it will feel like an itchy burn. Note to self: don't step until I see what's below.

I make it to the bottom, as the boys are already playing on the sandbar with their parents. But wait! You see all of this mushy green stuff, like a weird seaweed, that you have to walk through to get to the sandbar then Pacific Ocean. No one told me that, as you can't see it from the top of the cliff. I change my sneakers and put on my sandals and slowly move above the "kelp." It's only a few inches thick, but is slimy and reminds me of the bottom of a fish tank. Eeeww! I make it to the sand and see these gorgeous shells. They are sand dollars, pure white, with a fancy design the sea has created. It is so magical! Made by God.

The family that lives on the island tell me how breakable they are, but I am welcome to take as many as I want! I put a few in my sneakers inside of the bag I brought. People are scattered everywhere. By people, I mean the families of four adults and seven kids. Some in the ocean and others on the sand. I walk a bit, alone, and am reminded of the "Footprints in the Sand" poem. No idea why, but I just did. My feet touch the warm and murky water.

SHOELESS

As it trickles around my feet, I stop and look ahead of me. Even though I have travelled to some gorgeous places with this family, this is indeed the most peaceful and beautiful spot I've ever been. The Olympic mountains are right in front of me, with the oceans warm water at my feet. I decide to try and pray. I'm usually not so spiritual, but I feel different all over my body. I smile and offer thanksgiving for all of my blessings. I think this is the actual moment I "found God." I know, it sounds tacky, but a combination of all of the teachers I've been watching on Oprah's Super Soul Sunday's along with a lifetime of Masses and homilies, I see it. Well, not really see it, but feel it within. Something has entered me. No, I feel my Spirit inside. I can now live like never before. I get it! I wish Matt were here to join me. I pick up another sand dollar shell.

I pull out my phone and hope to photograph all, or at least some, of this beauty, but my phone is acting strangely. As I power it on, it turns itself off. Then immediately powers itself back on and says something about "Reloading all Photos." What the heck? I have over 1,300 of them. As this occurs, a humungous, loud, black helicopter flies in front of me over the ocean. Looks almost military and not private. The nanny family parents walk by me and jokingly say, "They have found you! What are you wanted for?" Like right! This family is so funny. I later find out that there is a Naval Air Station on Whidbey Island. Maybe that's why I had such terrible reception on my phone.

As the parents walk by, I remember that I didn't pack my sunscreen to reapply. I ask how long they were planning on staying down here and after they said a few hours, I asked if I could go back upstairs for my private time. I was determined not to get a sunburn, plus my allergies and cough were killing me. They obliged and were happy to see that I actually made it down here. They are such nice people. Truthfully, I wanted and needed more "me time."

It wasn't the "getting down here" that was as difficult, it was returning to the top. By now, the tide has started to come in as I walk to the ladder.

The bottom of the fish tank kelp stuff is now up to my knees. Yuck! It was so goopy, icky, just Yuck! But I treaded through and then had to hoist myself up the ladder. I am so grateful that I am down about 25 pounds or this would have never happened. I'd have been stuck, swallowed up by the sea as the tide came in. Just kidding!

Three hundred steps up, and dodging the leaves that will kill you, I make it to the first manmade rest area. I take a chance and see that my phone is now working. I call the "Love of my Life" and he answers! He hasn't left yet for his trip! I explain my predicament and I ask that he be with me in more than spirit. I place my phone in my cleavage, on speaker and start back up.

I talk, he talks, I say the "little engine that could" mantra for a while. I can still hear Matt. As I climb each step, I soon forget about the killer weeds and I got stung! It burns but I am determined not to scratch it, as per instructed earlier today. I don't know if I can make it. I'm getting out of breath. Oh! A snake crosses my path where the steps are covered in grass. It was probably less than a foot long, but a snake is a snake in my book! I scream and run up the hill. Panting and wheezing, along with coughing uncontrollably, I get to the back porch and get the phone out of my sweaty breasts. "I did it!" I proclaim to Matt. "I love you honey," he says, "and I will see you in two weeks. My plane is about to board." He was with me after all. Damn, I forgot to take pictures!

The flight home was quite eventful for me. We had to stop in San Francisco to change planes, and as I look out of my window as we descend the airport, I see the Asiana Airlines flight 214 plane outside of my window. It was just a few days ago, on this very tarmac that it crashed. I'll never forget this sight. When we arrived, the dad had to get on a different flight for business, and the mom and I had the four kids to ourselves. Only this time my eyes were so swollen from the allergies on the island, that it looked like I was either beaten up or had plastic surgery gone wrong.

As soon as I arrive home, I call my doctor. I get the last appointment of the day with a doctor that I haven't met before today. My doctor, of many years, was booked. Feel like crap. Look like crap. I'm happy Matt doesn't see me this way. I am given antibiotics, eye drops, different inhaler, a bunch of stuff. Someone will call me next week to set up a pulmonary functions test to check my lungs. I hope I can live that long.

I now have six weeks off! Paid! Those sometime fifty plus hour weeks were worth it! The Nanny Family goes to Europe...

Except that week one basically spent itching, all over. The antibiotics gave me a yeast infection! I eat tons of yogurt. Plus, more meds.

Matt Skype's me on our normal Sunday time and explains he has to stay an extra week, but will meet me at our restaurant for my birthday lunch. I was actually okay about this, as I really wanted to look great and feel better when I saw him.

SHOELESS

"...hell, I can't get you out of my head..."
-Florida Georgia Line, Cruise

The next week was filled with more "firsts" for me. My baby girl and I were headed to Atlanta for a "Couponers Meet-Up." We have not done anything like this together since probably Girl Scouts, and now she is 21. We are meeting the man that taught me had to do multiple transactions at Wags! A little over a year ago I spent $19 out-of-pocket, mostly tax, and got $252 worth of merchandise with their Register Rewards! Since then, we have couponed for tons of free or moneymaking stuff. A television at Rite Aid, Adirondack chairs from Harris Teeter (using Wags RR), basically anything CVS sells, Target gift cards, and the Wal-Mart with their cash back, ALL FREE! So, I just want to say "Thank you! YOU'RE THE DUDE! YOU HAVE CHANGED MY FAMILY'S LIFE!"

The car ride should have taken around six hours, but with rain, Atlanta traffic, and getting lost, it took eight. Didn't see much of the city going in, as it was thundering and looked like a monsoon was hitting us. We had the best mother-daughter time! Laughing, singing songs from the radio, and even had a car pass us and stick his arm out the window and made the wolf sign to us (North Carolina plates, and we have a UNC sticker on the back of the car. In all fairness, also a Duke Alum sticker, as Matt graduated from there. We are a house divided.).

We got to meet so many in the couponing community that I admire. The electricity went out and we still had a great time. The MC even went around the room and introduced those of us with YouTube Channels, even little me, with only 260 subs!

SHOELESS

We stayed at a nearby hotel and I watched the evening news. A missing girl from the area was shown. I swear these missing girls are looking so familiar. But how? She's from Georgia.

My daughter and I do something so out of character for us. Instead of going straight home, I have her pick anywhere she wants to stop and visit. The World of Coca Cola it is! Normally we would visit a museum or something historical if her dad was here. Funny though, I haven't had a soda pop since 2012! They had an entire room to taste drinks from all over the world made by Coca-Cola. (May I suggest you skip the 'Beverly' from Italy?)

The vacation time was filled with fun trips and activities!

Another first. I went to an all-women's day long retreat that the diocese put on. I have not been on any retreats for myself since 1985 for Teens Encounter Christ and I had to travel to Omaha, Nebraska from Boca Raton, Florida. Life was too busy with four kids! I guess that I never made time for me.

SHOELESS

Something miraculous, yes, that's the term to use, has happened to me, just two days before my birthday. I have been searching for so long for answers to my faith. Listening attentively at mass each Sunday, and really trying to fit the puzzle pieces together. At this morning retreat, I was able to really concentrate on my life. I think that it was the "healing waters" that I was sent to in Washington and finally saw God. God is all around us. Not just a Bible passage or activity. God is in everything and everyone that we encounter. The retreat was titled, *Come, all of you that are thirsty.* I am ever so grateful for those experiences. From meditating at "the woman at the well" to the "shell meditation." We were able to share in our small groups and I actually think that I made sense. Before the Pacific Ocean, I didn't "get it." I think I was finally ready. Receiving the shell brought me back to Whidbey Island. That's where I found God. However, I was not able to bring myself to go to confession that was available there. What would I say? I went to New York, with a man from my past, not my husband, nothing happened, and I

SHOELESS

am hiding a lot of cash in our house. I feel like a
fraud. I'm ashamed in my dishonesty. But I just keep
smiling throughout this day.

SHOELESS

"I belong with you, you belong with me,
you're my sweetheart..."
-The Lumineers, <u>Ho Hey</u>

I didn't get my Sunday night telephone call from Mexico. I try not to worry. We have come this far. I wake up alone on my 46th birthday, filled with anticipation. I drive down to Millbrook Road and head to Assaggio's. As I walk in, I ask for a table for two, look up and see my husband at our favorite table! Love-n-hugs! We catch up, and I'm told that he can't stay an extra week to bring our son back to Texas. So, I agree to take the two-day drive and have our son all to myself.

SHOELESS

Something seems different about Matt. Maybe he's just tired from the flight. When we arrive home, he goes to bed until the next morning. So, I catch up on my couponing. Kroger will have some sweet Gillette deals later this week. I haven't put out a video since Atlanta, so I want to make this good for my subscribers. Funny, I really do this out of the want for helping others. I do not make money and show advertisements before each video.

That weekend, Matt and I go to our first couples retreat since our engagement. It was held at the same church I went to a few weeks ago. It felt good to reconnect. Maybe it's not Matt that I see the changes, but myself and guilt. How could I tell him? Why would I tell him? Even though I have money from this, I don't think he'd trust me having a "double life." I try to justify my actions in that I haven't a clue what he does in Mexico. It's not that I don't care, I just know he would say that I have a wild imagination.

It's "Super Soul Sunday," and I sleep in long enough to catch the full episode before it hits the

DVR. How I love watching Oprah. I really have to personally thank her for helping me become the woman that I am today. Yes, like that will ever happen. Deepak Chopra is Oprah's guest today. Something about a 21 Day Meditation. Wow! How I could use this right now! I register online. I hope I can accomplish this thing called meditation. My mind roams too much and my head is full of clutter. Well, it officially begins tomorrow.

Our family trip is a blast. The kids all meet up at the house and we drive to the mountains. This is our first family trip in a long time. And it is fun. Not Forced Family Fun! We have two in college and two out of college, so schedules and logistics has always been a challenge these past few years. We stayed at Beech Mountain and had some good old-fashioned family fun.

We even stop on the side of the Blue Ridge Parkway and I surprised the kids. They said they want to do a hike and follow a trail. I agree to join! This is the first time in their lifetime that they saw me attempt something like this. I used to be inactive, because of my weight, laziness and depression, plus I worried all the time. We ended up at the top of this mountains rocky cliff and experienced the clouds going through us. It is so peaceful. I am so proud of myself!

Matt and I stayed an extra night after the kids went home or elsewhere. It was a magical night. Maybe because we were in the mountains. I know it sounds strange, but even after being together for almost three decades, I don't think we have lost our special intimacy. It just seemed different. My guilt? But I haven't been with Zaran since he reentered my life. Yet. It just seems hard to imagine actually living a perfect world of travelling, expensive gifts, homes all over the world...

On the way home, we stopped at a Cracker Barrel for lunch. I noticed an older woman sitting alone. How sad. I really wanted to go and ask her to join us. When I told Matt, we compromised and agreed just to pay for her lunch. A simple act of kindness, but it felt right.

SHOELESS

We actually have a full Saturday to get things done around the house. Caulking the shower project has been put on hold because my cough is getting worse, and my kidney stone feels like it could pass soon. How many weeks of pain was it this time? I don't even keep track anymore.

SHOELESS

"When I'm gone, When I'm gone,
You're gonna miss me when I'm gone…"
-Anna Kendrick, Cups

I go to bed early and am awakened by Matt loudly pulling the bathroom door open and stating, "I love you." I was about to reply, but he continues, and I figure he is on the phone with someone, "I'll be right downstairs Angel. You're early," as he runs out of our bedroom door.

I sit up and boldly state, "You love, who?" and realize that he is now going down the stairs, leaving me without even a kiss goodbye, hurrying outside to meet a woman he said he loves. And it wasn't me.

As he is about to open the front door to leave, I am in the landing and he looks up stating, "It's just Angela, my ride to the airport. Our flight leaves in less than an hour. I was just joking about the love thing, as I didn't want her angry at me for not being ready on time. She's always late. I love you, see you in a few weeks, I'll Skype you later." And with that, and no kiss goodbye, he leaves our once happy home. I go down the stairs and look out the window. It's the ravenous beauty he hugged at the airport that time.

I decide to go back to bed, it's 3:30 in the morning.

I sleep in, not even getting my multiple copies of the Sunday newspaper for the coupons. I am utterly confused. It's all in my mind, I'm overthinking again, or am I just gullible for his charm? I know "everybody" loves Matt.

I'll keep busy. Time to organize the house. Time to coupon. I only have a few more weeks off of work. This house needs a lot done to it. Maybe I can buy a new central air conditioning unit with my extra cash in the shoebox. Even negotiate a discount for paying by cash. No, Matt will know immediately! Ugh! All of this money and maybe I'll use it for little repairs. We have a long list. I wish I could write Suze Orman and ask her for financial advice. Already know her answer: eliminate debt, have at least eight months of an emergency fund, and get that retirement fund growing. How would I not tell her that these extra funds are in cash. Why? Am I doing something illegal? Crap, how do I claim it on my taxes? Forget that, I still owe them a lot.

So much to do. I really try not to think about Matt. I guess I always thought he worked 24/7 when he was away. "Truthiness" has been my way of thinking. I might be changing my ways. Come to think of it, he is traveling and extending his travel plans. That woman, Angela, or did he have a nickname, Angel, that I heard him call her too?

These past few months, complete with my extracurricular activities, though not sexual, is making me rethink my life. Or am I overthinking again? Yes, I think when I was getting the warm water from the Pacific Ocean pour over my feet, I "found" God, at least a better understanding or openness about my life. I am here for a reason. I just need to figure out the details!

My coughing seems a lot worse, almost unbearable at times. Plus, I am itchy all over. Why hasn't my doctor called back with a follow-up appointment? Then, the doorbell rings and a huge bouquet of expensive flowers arrive on my doorstep. I hold it up so that I can see the bottom of it and yes, it's a heavy Waterford crystal vase. No card. Oh, Matt! He must feel awful about how he left this morning. I can't remember the last time he spent so much money on me.

I decide to pack a suitcase for my trip with one of my sons this week. He works in Texas, let's just say "on a special assignment." But you can figure that out later. Another first, a road trip from

Raleigh, North Carolina, to the Texas/Mexican border! I will fly home, and then fly back to New York City for my second photo session.

I go to church, alone, and hear the priest's homily. Father Bob doesn't want us to be bystanders. I'll remember that if it comes up in my life.

As soon as I arrive home, my Skype account is ringing on my computer. Matt must be calling to apologize! I hear the connection and see Matt's head quickly swivel around his chair to see in back of him. A woman is in the background, apparently just walking into his room, and announces, "Guess what I brought for you?" as she is holding something behind her back. Only her front is what has me puzzled. This young brunette has two long braids that are barely covering her nipples and it looks like she isn't wearing a top. She walks closer to my husband. Yes, she is indeed topless. Plus, a towel is wrapped around her from her midsection down, exposing her bellybutton ring.

SHOELESS

My husband jokingly replies, "a shirt for you to put on?"

She giggles. She continues using an awful vocal cry voice, "We're going down to the pond to bathe, why would I need a top? No, I brought us new soap! Remember, we lost it on our last trip!" What?!? Bathe? Together? I thought this was a modest place and there are two separate areas for men and woman? Did she say last trip, he's done this before? Then Mystery Boobs notices me looking at her on the computer screen and starts to walk closer to the screen, Matt turns around and sees me, and she bends and leans her left breast against my husband's back shoulder and chimes in to have a conversation with me onscreen. Now her right braid has moved into her armpit and her bare breast is in my full view. Matt's too, if he views the lower screen or moves his head.

"Well, hi! I'm Angela, well, Angel, as Matthew likes to call me. I'm his assistant. You must be Cat; I've heard so much about you!" Really? I've only heard her name mentioned once, during the "I love you" incident at 3:30 earlier this morning. Matt looks like a deer has hit him with the headlights! Matt must have just realized that our phone connection was active and I've seen everything, including her nipple. He has a strange look on his face and is speechless. His expression is a combination of guilt and terror. He should feel both, because I'm about to make his life a living hell! This isn't going to be an apology phone call. He says absolutely nothing to me.

Bouncing boobs girl, I mean Angela, continues, rather quickly, "Sorry to interrupt, I thought Matt was done with his call to you. He is such a lifesaver here!" I'm thinking sure, he's a PA, he saves lives. But then she adds, "We used to have to walk for over a mile to get to the lake to bathe in two separate areas. Matt found a secluded pond just minutes from here! It's so much easier." Now she takes her right hand and collects her ponytail, pushing her breast against my husband. "I figure, he's seen me topless each time we venture to the beach, so what's removing a few more inches of material and strings. We see bodies all the time in this profession. I'm not a prude."

Were my facial expressions of utter madness showing yet? I could feel my anger about to blow. I take another deep breath. Matt quickly interrupted "Angel…a, can I have a few words with my wife. Alone? Please?" She pulls away from him exposing both breasts to me, and at Matt's eye level, however, not fazing Matt, as he has definitely seen them before.

"No, wait, finish your story. Matt, don't interrupt, I don't want to miss a detail and be, what do you call it, 'I overthink everything'," I suggest. With great anticipation, not, I smirk at him. Her breasts are filling the screen more than him. I try not to stare at her perky, huge, perfectly globe shaped rounds. But shit, she has the exact Pandora necklace that he just gave me for my birthday!

Then she said the best part, "And he is great with soap!"

She is then interrupted with Matt's, "No, stop!"

In which I say loudly, "Let this topless girl finish." Calmly, I begin with: "I know; I've been showering with him longer than you've been alive!" and I gave him a look from hell. I wonder, is she naked under that towel?

"You have such a giving husband. He is such a great mentor. He's taught me a lot. He's given me self-confidence. Even at the beach, **he said I was beautiful**! He is so nice! And to top it off, no pun intended, he took a photo of me playing on the beach. You know how he is always sending pics on his phone."

Yeah, I can honestly say that he didn't send that one to me! I think, for a twenty-something year old, she is either really naive, or she is playing me like a pro. Yup, pro she is. She has almost carefully staged every bounce during this phone call. Then she hugs him, giggling and jiggling, pushing her tits against him. By his expression again, it still doesn't look the first time this has happened. Matt kind of pushes her off of him.

With that annoying vocal cry, she continues, "I can't wait to meet you. Maybe we can all get together back in Raleigh. I see you two in Church together all the time." Then she stands and turns to Matt, breasts at his mouth level, collects both braids to try and cover her nipples, does a stupid bite of her lip, innocent look to Matt, pulls her ponytails together down her cleavage, squeezing both arms closer to her body, thus exaggerating the size of her breasts to me and showing my husband both of her now erect nipples. What the hell is she talking about? Get together? Conniving bitch. Yes, bitch is the term. Excuse my language. No, don't excuse it. I'm sick of being the good wife! I wish I could reach my hands through the computer screen and choke her to death. I don't give a damn about The Ten Commandments right now.

I have never seen his face like this before. Caught in the cookie jar full of breasts? She begins to turn and bounce her way out of his room. "Wait dear!" I announce. I stop to see if Matt will interject some thought of this situation. Nothing. Defending himself? Nothing. Begging for forgiveness? Nothing. Okay, like I told him in the past, he'd be history. But I forgot to tell him there would be a price. He can't win.

So here I go...starting with my nice, understated, old ball and chains attitude, "Angela, bless your heart, you young naive, little thing." Now my voice is getting louder, "You may think that I'm too old and stupid to play this game. Honey, I can beat you blindfolded and with a turtleneck on." Quick pause, wondering how I am coming up with this stuff. "Sure, your tits are right there in his face, and he will probably play, or continue to play with you as long as he can get away with it. Trust me: you're not the first extra set he's had." Waiting for Matt to interrupt that I am lying, he doesn't. So, I'm right! His silence gave it away! He looked stunned, not defending, not saying anything. Does he think this is a dream and he can't talk? Whatever. I brainwashed myself in thinking we were happy together. At least until this year, when he started to go away and save the world. Some humanitarian. I was always giving him the benefit of the doubt. Just thinking I had a wild or perverted imagination. But as I learned from Oprah, having a gut feeling. This was that feeling. A sixth sense. All of those texts he did on the couch he thought I didn't notice. The bringing the phone in the bathroom or his closet. Bringing his phone everywhere. Not sharing his passwords to anything. Everyone else said we were the perfect family. Life went on, and I actually fell in love with him again, well, in my mind, over the last few years as the kids started to leave and we could reconnect. He was hiding something, or someone. Little hints I tried to ignore or compensate with lies to myself. An audible sigh, almost sadness in my voice. My accelerated grieving is over and my pissed tone comes to life.

"Well bitch, you can have him and his many debts. And, I do know about how great he is with soap, as he soaped me up all over inside and out just two nights ago!" (She looks pissed, as she was probably told the proverbial "my wife and I haven't had sex in years crap" from any husband!) Then I get her with, "Oh, and I'd check for STDs if I were you. And expect a letter from my lawyer upon your return. It's still illegal to play games with a married man from North Carolina. Suing you will be such fun! Bless your heart!" I add a certain look...

She turns and walks out, also dropping her towel to show me her naked ass onscreen. She wasn't even looking at my soon to be castrated husband.

Uncharacteristic of me, I now say nothing. He looks at me. He's speechless? That has never happened in decades.

"I'm sorry," he barely says audibly.

To my reply, with attitude, "For what exactly are you sorry? For spending your free time at topless beaches, in which, one, I didn't know you had free time in your busy schedule, or two, that I caught you with a naked, toweled woman? Who, come to think of it, is probably about our daughter's age, anyway, and neither of you denied an affair."

My head is spinning with many thoughts, "And you have always acted so prim and proper, never wanting to go to places like that with me. Always having me cover up, even in our house so the next-door neighbors couldn't see. Or are you sorry that I had the pleasure of hearing a probable fantasy come true of my husband of soaping up another woman. If that's all you did."

"Okay that's enough. We can talk about this when I get home in a little over a week. You're overthinking this. You always overthink things. I see parts of the body all the time. You know that, it's what I do. The body is a…"

"Don't give me that bullshit." I've never talked to my husband like this moment. My language has diabolically changed since this videophone call. For most of our marriage I have believed him, in various instances like the time he "had to go to the topless bar" because his friend had never experienced it, and I was out of town. Only I didn't find out until his friend's girlfriend told me months later. Sure, that was "medical." I got over several things throughout our married life, but this takes the cake.

"Or are you sorry for something else?" I don't know what came over me. Maybe years of trying to avoid conflict. Being the good wife. Keeping quiet.

"Do I have to investigate if you have an Ashley Madison account?" His look is clueless, but I gained this information thanks to television! I now know quite a bit! "Or have you been playing the Petraeus email draft game? I doubt you "friended" her on Facebook, as that could open another can of worms. Her status probably says 'It's complicated.'" Then I give a little revenge laugh, and continue, almost babbling, but sharing my almost senseless but meaningful knowledge.

"You know, I could write a hot novel, slip some of this in, of course, changing enough names and places, so you wouldn't sue me for slander. I'd, of course, hide this storyline because the main story will be of some important issue of our day. Or you could sue me, but then word would spread like wildfire causing people to believe me or even doubt you anyways. Trust me, if the former Director of the CIA can't get away with this, and you only have an undereducated, poor "little ole me" wife that has pretty much loved you faithfully for most of her life, trying to figure this out. But then I'd need proof, let's see, oh, wait!"

I'm actually laughing in my head, "I can see you with both Jon Stewart and Stephen Colbert in a rare joint television interview, pointing his left finger on his *Wag of the Finger* saying, *So, we hear you were Skyping your wife from Mexico and then your hot young topless mistress walks in. (They give their looks.) In what universe did you think this would end up well?* Or you can make Ellen's show as one of her pictures of the day. Can't wait for that monologue! Ohhhh! Wendy Williams, "*howyadoin*" and her audience will cremate you." I pause and just look at him.

Then my mind hurries to another option! I could be promoting this book with the ladies on *The*

View. Sherry Shepherd would start with, "I know this book is about such an important worldwide issue (I guess I should research an actual issue!), but let me start with the *Skype Chapter*. I gotta say, at first, I thought that you were too kind with that bitch (they bleep the word!), as I would have been in her face with a louder attitude, cause you all know me. Well, you certainly stuck it to him! Then Whoopi will continue with asking: So, the whole world wants to know, why did you write this book? And my coded answer for revenge will simply be, "to get out of debt." Then I turn and look into the camera like a close-up of Mr. Roper on an old episode of Three's Company, smirking! The entire audience will give a loud standing ovation, as they catch my coded answer! Barbara Walters will ask if any of this book is true, and Sherry will tell her that I just gave her that answer with my smirk! Tears and high fives everywhere! Oh, I wish Joy Behar was still on, then I could personally thank her for introducing me to the term *Skinny Bitch!*

Snapping back to reality, as my ADHD has taken over, even here! Matt is still silent, even after my daydreaming! "This good Catholic wife has been a little busy being educated on this Skype thing and more. I do thank you for teaching me how to set it up and the few things I know about this computer technology."

Here come my punch lines: "Did you know that you can do so much besides talk here? I also learned a lot about the power of social media and how quickly news travels. Maybe I can start with our church friends, with pictures of your trips and what you do in your free time. I know, people will call me a scornful woman by her words. Maybe I'll add a picture or two. If a picture is worth a thousand words, this one will speak to more than that! No, not one of the dozens we all have of you with your arm around women in group photos from all of your travels. Your "Angel" is probably in some of these. Is your arm around that tramp you just had in your room?"

I give a slight mysterious, "watch your ass" pause, continuing, "Oh, I mean, a picture from several minutes ago. But let's see, did you know you can take and freeze photos from this Skype thing? I taught myself on this fact. I have one of her walking in, a closer one with her right breast off your side, her filling the screen closer up, her standing up turned towards your mouth. And did you see her ass as she walked out of your room as she dropped her towel? I have that saved too. Didn't think you liked big butts. Oh, the choices! Just tell me, why? I gave you everything. Did you already take her to," and before I could say "bed" I saw him shake his head and press the "END CALL" key. Phone call over. I think he purposefully turned it off, it wasn't because of a bad connection. Here I go again, giving him the benefit of doubt. GAME OVER! What? Really?

After all of that, with Miss Bouncing Slut Boobs, I remember most vividly she said my husband called her "beautiful." He still never did that to me even after I gave him the story from the stranger in McDonald's. Some stranger he turned out to be. I'll think about it. I've been the "Good Girl" for a long while now. And I remember how Zaran is not so good, but is very, very good! This Catholic woman is really screwed up. I pick up the heavy vase and scream like I've never screamed before in my life and throw the flowers across the room, shattering it against the wall. I fall to the floor in a fetal position. Why is this happening?!?

I really meant it when I told him through the years that I wasn't going to fight for him. Paybacks, however, watch out, I'm a redhead! That legal comment was just to throw the bitch off a bit. Boy, has my language changed! Maybe it's my thoughts of possibilities with Zaran that has taken over my hopes. Money, travelling, fancy everything. Hey, if that love thing got me where I am today, I am open to possibilities. Even if I don't really know him. I thought I knew my husband.

SHOELESS

"Show me how to fight for now..."
-Justin Timberlake, <u>Mirrors</u>

I try to start Day 9 with my new 21-day Daily Meditation. I've done this religiously for eight days in a row! I can usually even concentrate, I mean meditate, and stop my busy thoughts. Are Catholics allowed to do this? Meditate, I mean? I still don't know all of the rules. I'm kind of mixing a bunch of stuff when it comes to my spirituality. Catholic Church member that meditates and chants, and faithfully follow Oprah's "Super Soul Sunday" guests in learning about discovering my inner self and life's purpose. I save the email and will try again later.

Last evening's call has me flustered. That's not the right word. There is no word to describe how I feel. I'll let him see if he can weasel his way out of this mess when he returns in a few weeks. Maybe it was me and my breast issues. Thinking about it, I grew up with hypocritical parents. Holier-than-thou church goers and prayer groups, but also hiding porn and other stuff. Breasts were deemed taboo…until my visit to the Bahamas. I have to shelf this issue with Matt and wait until his return next week. Whatever happened either has or hasn't. No sense stroking out on it. Let me concentrate on my son for the next few days. Then of course, my own secret life. Really? I can admit it. I'm leading a double life. My friends in the church pews have no idea. Good little Catholic that I am. Not!

My oldest son and I head out at 7 a.m. for his work in Texas. The car is packed with stuff he will need. I am not sure where we are going, let alone how we will get there, but am up for this mother-son adventure! I take the first driving shift. I-540 to I-40 to 85 South. Just the way my daughter and I went to Atlanta! (Oh, that reminds me, I have to remember to send some Wags booklets to my fellow couponers I met there.) After a lunch break, we change drivers. He has me look on my phone how to get out of Atlanta, as I missed the I-85 turn. Our first argument. I had the maps on the phone, and then lost the little blue directional dot! How do you find where you are? We pull over, I had a quick lesson, and proceeded on. My son is baffled that it was only a few years ago I ran my own company, and now I can't read a map! To which I immediately told him I can read a real printed map. Can his generation do that job? Off we go!

At the rest stop in Alabama, I pick up some area brochures, as you never know when you'll be back, along with an interesting card. It was a folded business card stating: **Help Stop Modern Day Slavery.** This gray card has a Quick Guide to Identifying Victims. Also, if you suspect someone of being trafficked, what to do and a **National Human Trafficking Hotline.** I doubt I will ever use this number in my drab life.

SHOELESS

I fall asleep as we drive through Mississippi. Before we know it, we are in Louisiana and try and find our hotel. My genius son has searched for the exact directions on the phone, quite specific in letting us know the length in feet for when to turn. That app was so terribly wrong in that it sent us down a dark road to nowhere. Literally. Just a dead end with barely enough room to turn around. Technology, my ass.

The hotel we stayed at had just been updated. It even had another television screen in the bathroom! After a somewhat uneasy night, I had weird dreams from Matt with that slut, to a kaleidoscope of various children's images.

We got on the road early, but I did catch a glimpse of the area news. Another alert of a teenage girl that has been missing for a few months. They showed a school picture. Why are these kids starting to all look alike to me? I don't know them.

We forgot to fuel up before leaving, so we stopped at an Official Rest Stop. It was actually off of one of the longest bridges I had ever been on.

SHOELESS

Down we went, on a dusty, almost unpaved looking graveled over road to get to the stop. Crap, the gas station locator sign says it is many miles down the swamp land. No thanks. I saw too many alligators up close and personal while riding bicycles in Kiawah a few months ago.

I did have to use the ladies' room, though, so we stopped at the center. Just a quick stop. I went into the ladies' room, and closed the stall. I hear the toilet flush next to me and see two smaller shoeless feet. Strange for a bathroom.

I finish, walk to the sinks and see a young blonde teenager walk out of the bathroom. Doesn't she know it's not safe to walk around without shoes? Of course, I'm still in mother/nanny mode. Back out in the car, we start to drive away on the now barely graveled road. At the other end of the parking lot, near the truck stop area, I see the young teen open a van door. I'll never forget the white cargo van with no windows on the side, but when opened had an old, brown blanket covering the door area. As this girl pulls the shaggy blanket back to enter, another girl, Hispanic looking, gets out. She is shoeless too. Both seem really skinny and dirty.

"Stop!" I said to my son.

He hadn't seen what I saw. Quick explanation, and he says, "Mom, many people live out of their cars during exhibition season." I don't know what he is talking about. Plus, of all the television shows I watch, I haven't seen the ones about the people and the swamp. "Mom," he touches my hand, "they are probably not homeless." We leave the parking area and head back up the bridge. I say a special prayer.

It's still on my mind. Homeless? I wasn't even thinking of that scenario. I open my wallet and got out the folded business card on human trafficking that I picked up earlier today. It doesn't say anything about kids without shoes. Should I call the number? I'm trying to rationalize what I saw. They could be sisters. I too have blondes and darker skinned kids. Uggggh! We stop for gas. He tells me not to get out of the car. Safety? Shouldn't I be protecting him? Oh, I want to call that hotline. But

I do seem to overthink everything. I am not part of a Lifetime movie. I'm just a nanny. Right now, just a mom on a car trip with her adult son. Another prayer for safety for these two little souls. A police car pulls up for gas. My son is still pumping gas. I get out and tell the officer what I saw. He has his partner call something in on their phones.

There. I did something. I was not a bystander. Fr. Bob would be proud. I heard and responded to his homily. The officer didn't even look at me like I was a nut case. I can breathe. I hope that I was wrong. I hope those two girls are safe.

We head down the road and I see a white cargo van with no side windows. Was this the van saw earlier? Did the police miss it? I never saw license plate number. Ohhhhhhhhh! I'm frustrated. I'm in the passenger's seat this time look at the driver. White, balding, overweight, tir looking older guy in a light lime green ratty old shirt. They speed up and I never see them ag How does a person profile a Human Trafficker?

151

search the web later. I'm tired and sleepy. I'm trying not to overthink things.

Sometime later we made it to Texas. As we pass Sugarland, Texas, I almost ask my son if this is the place where the show "The Client List" is based. I decide to keep my mouth shut, as he will probably think I use too much valuable time watching trashy shows.

One thing I will add is that Texas takes a hell-of-a-long-time to drive across. Ten hours or so to our destination! And mind you, EVERYONE is going at least 85 mph on this barren stretch of highway land. There is nothing but land, everywhere you look. We make it to our location, which you can figure out later, at almost midnight. It seems too dangerous to drive here alone at night. The Border Patrol is everywhere.

I sleep for a few hours until daylight. Then I hug and kiss my son goodbye, after we visit an authentic Mexican restaurant for breakfast. I wish him good luck in this tiny border town, and drive right to McAllen Airport.

SHOELESS

"I can show you love
In a tidal wave of mystery
You'll still be standing next to me..."
-Capital Cities, <u>Safe and Sound</u>

I arrive home from Texas just in time to clean some clothes and repack. My mind cannot stop about the two girls in the van. I look again at the little gray folded business card about Human Trafficking. I can't make up my mind if I should call the number.

Oh, my husband didn't come home early either to defend himself or even fight for our marriage. This action says it all. Is it too late? I'm not sure of my next steps to take regarding Matt or Zaran. So, I quickly decide. Then I change my mind. I'm so ADHD. So many things to consider.

I finally decide that I'm going for an overnighter in New York City! Before the 'Topless Angela rubbing her breast against my husband's back and hugs him' incident, I would have been more nervous about this trip. But two can play this game. I don't really believe that, but I'm so confused right now. Maybe if Zaran makes a move, but do I want to ruin my marriage? Maybe Matt didn't. He is a good man. But then again, he is a man. My life with Matt isn't a game. But the whole thing pisses me off. I'll see him in a week. Maybe he will call on Sunday night. I'll be home by then. Am I overthinking things again?

After my flight, a limo picks me up at the airport and we drive for just a bit. The limo driver stops in front of the Four Seasons Hotel and I am instructed to take the elevator to the 32nd floor. A doorman opens the door to the Grand Lobby. It is beyond spectacular. The elevator doors open and

Zaran greets me with a sexy smile, and those big, brown eyes, and a huge, tight hug, along with an apology for missing my arrival at the airport. He asks me if I liked the flowers he sent. I smile. Oh, no! I'm mixing up men!

As we enter the 32nd floor, we have a three bedroom that has balconies and views of both the city and Central Park. The shades are even electronic. So many little things this poor country girl is unaccustomed to viewing (I'm trying to make a joke.). "Catie, I must also apologize that the photography session has been postponed." I was misled.

"Zaran, you could have called me. Is everything alright?" I am puzzled. Then why am I here?

He continues," I hope you are not disappointed, but now I can have you for an entire twenty-four hours." Oh, Lord, I remember what twenty-four hours was to this man almost thirty years ago. I am hypnotized by Zaran's presence.

I look up at him, straight into his sexy brown eyes and say, "I don't want to disappoint you, but I am married and I've been pretty faithful to my husband" with his "Be that as it may" I abruptly stop him and say, "No, *be that as it may,"* and he takes my hand, walks me out to the balcony and says, "I want to show you my American City. I have homes in all parts of the world. You are welcome to join me … when you are ready. I want to be with my someone special, you Catie, and grow old together. I can give you anything you want. Do you remember any of our conversation on the cruise?" As he proclaims this, he hands me a box. A rather large box with a satin ribbon on it. It occurs to me that I don't know much about this man.

"Thank you for the gifts, but you really don't know me. You had me a long time ago, and I have changed."

With that said he says optimistically, "Open the box. I know what you like." I slowly untie the ribbon, and begin to open it. It's the blue designer dress that my friend "T" had made (She is a fellow couponer from Jamaica, New York, that I found on YouTube). Zaran responds with a "You commented about it on Facebook." This is weird. He's creeping on me on Facebook! "I also got you the coral nightgown she designed, too. I can get you everything my Darling. She can be your custom personal fashion designer. I want to show you the world. I've made my riches, now I want to have someone, no not just someone, you, to enjoy them with." I am shocked.

We sit down to a glass of wine. My mind is spinning. I only take a few sips.

"Why are you on my Facebook? I can't even find you when I Google you." I pause and look into those dreamy dark eyes again. He's still not clean shaven, but hot.

"I made my wealth through helping those in need of the law. Worldwide. I get the job done. I always finish what I start. We started almost thirty years ago." That seemed ominous. Oh shit, why am I here? "Come, let's go walk around Central Park," pointing outside, "then we have an early dinner reservation. He brings my bag to a gorgeous room and hangs up my new dress. In the right size. How? Only this is the dress that she designed before she covered the chest area, thinking it was a mistake in the pattern. Oh, thank God, there's a piece of material I think covers my breasts. At least I hope it will cover my breasts! "This is your room when we are here. Mine is across the dining area, when you are ready. No pressure. I just know you will want me later," showing me a confident, ever appealing look of lust.

I am so confused. What's new? This space is huge! Beautifully decorated in ivory colors. I try reminding myself I'm married. To a possible adulterer, but still married. Just currently hate the man, and his "ANGEL." *Really, she couldn't have had another name? I'll never think of the "Angels above" that way again. Thanks bitch!*

It's a pretty mid-August Friday afternoon. As we walk, we view bicyclists, children playing, and a group just soaking up the sun reading. As we step closer, I notice that these readers are topless. Seriously!

"Is that legal?" I ask. You know, since seeing Zaran a few months ago, I start seeing topless women again. Before that, only in a few movies, but never up close, in my entire married life. Here we go again.

"Female toplessness is legal in any public space in New Your City. Do you want to take off your top now?" he asks so nonchalantly. "When we stay upstairs," pointing to the Four Seasons in back of us, "you can come down here anytime you want. Covered or uncovered. Come, let me help you remove your blouse. Just remember, I'm the only one that can touch, others can fantasize."

As I stop him, I think of the last time I was topless on the beach in the Bahamas, walking hand in hand. It was a different time, before camera phones and videos, and social media. Thank the Lord I was not photographed back then. I can't believe I tell him that my body has changed a lot in thirty years. His response was, "Show me and I'll be the judge of that," with a sly face. I remember hearing that self-confidence is sexy on a woman. So, if it were to happen, you know, I'll just pretend to own it. Even with having "stripes" from four pregnancies and all.

"Since seeing all of these topless women, just reading outside, can you please explain to me your male view of female breasts." I can't believe I asked him this. What the hell, I don't get it. He just matter-of-fact went on to explain that he was raised around Europe and that they are part of a woman's anatomy and are natural and meant to feed babies. So just lying around without covering them is not a big deal. It's more sexual when you see women prancing down the beach wearing a teeny string to cover ones' nipples, then get that suit wet, and have a nip slip, as if it were a surprise to her. Then she shows a little more by removing that material off her breast. It's all in the actions. Sex is in the mind and our imagination of what could or is happening is where the control is. If you are raised seeing them, even on television, it doesn't faze you the way you are teased in advertisements, or magazine spreads from an overly retouched women lit in romantic lighting that you know you can never have. Toplessness and sexuality are two different things. It wasn't until I came to the States that I was confused. You Americans are really screwed up." Well, it does kind of makes sense. I'm still not ready to undress in public.

"Why don't you want a young, perky thing to keep you occupied around the world?" I ask.

"I could pay for that, but honestly, I haven't forgotten you. We had an instant connection. You know what I mean. Soul to soul, almost thirty years ago. Since that moment on the cruise, you have always been a part of me. I don't need anyone younger as I don't necessarily want children," (Thank God, that factory is shut down!) "and I can spoil you. I want our relationship, the one we should have continued years ago."

"Why me?"

"I'll answer that later." He doesn't even know me now.

We continue walking, now hand in hand. He has a strong grip on me. We head toward the fountain and he turns to me, looks into my eyes, and I say, "Not here, please. Not yet." To which we started back to our suite.

I also found out that his client William will be stopping by to see us at dinner. He wants me to continue being his company's photographer whether or not I choose to build a relationship with Zaran.

How can I be thinking this way? I don't even know if Matt still wants to be married. Zaran is pretty vague about William's company, name, and all. I will ask him later at dinner.

As we head back upstairs, I notice how exquisitely the Four Seasons is designed. I'm not used to such elegance and how you are treated, more like, taken care of here. Taking care of, oh, my little Nanny Family, if I change my life, what will they do?

SHOELESS

Seriously. Why am I considering this? Again, my husband is with a ravenous young thing. My being perplexed is an understatement.

SHOELESS

If I fall for you, I'll never recover.
If I fall for you, I'll never be the same.
I really want to love somebody..."
-Maroon 5, Love Somebody

We each enter our own rooms to prepare for dinner. We are going to a place nearby called *Per Se.*

Before showering, I look for extra hidden cameras in the bathroom (thank you, Miss Erin Andrews!). Forget it. Somehow, he has access to my Facebook, so cameras are nothing. After bathing, I decide to try and act fancier than usual. I wrap my hair up off of my shoulders and braid it around in a fancy bun, loose curly hairs dangling around my face. Remembering the boobs and braids bitch, I redo my updo. I wish I had my Spanx! I put this gorgeous gown on, and like I remember commenting online to my Facebook friend, it was missing a piece in the front. My breasts were fully exposed. But I will say that the way it was originally designed, it helped push and lift them up. Full support! I did however, take the sheer floral material that was to cover my exposed area, so I folded it twice, as not to be sheer enough to show my nipples underneath. My couponing friend did a good job creating this dress! But Zaran saw my post about this dress on Facebook. Only seen by friends. How did he find out? He missed the post on how she corrected and added material to cover my front. Or did he? Does she know the dress is for me?

"Wow," he exclaimed as I entered the living room. Zaran twirled me around and placed me close to his tux. I still couldn't kiss him. That didn't mean that I did not want to, as this tall, wide, handsome, muscular man smelled ever so enticing. "Catie, you are about to enter an exclusive world. All of your desires can be fulfilled. You are going to meet the rest of my world. Just be open minded. I work with a very powerful woman, and she wants to not only meet you, but include you. This rarely occurs in my business."

I am so bewildered. "What are you talking about?"

"Catie, when you meet her, Chelseavonni, she might scare you with her boldness and the fact that she is a very sensual woman. Don't let her sex appeal baffle you. She's the head of our food chain. She has a specific reason to discuss your future plans together."

What? I interrupt with, "Is this sex? Or are the two of you…"

Zaran stops me, shaking his head. "No, no my darling, we were never lovers, but if you want her too, I will not stop you. I will fulfill all of your desires."

"Stop, this is too weird. Is tonight's dinner about this?"

Zaran replied, "Chelseavonni wants to include you in some details of our businesses. She will make it sound like you are in a tribunal. I'll explain later. Just listen. Then decide. I'll take you either way. She has some important work for you to accomplish. Once you enter the dining room, she is yours, as you are hers. Later, I am yours. Sexually yours, later. If you decide. You will. However, I am giving you the option. Who would turn me down?" Funny, I giggle, the guy has patience, that's for sure!

"Our dinner meeting is all work. She has done her homework on you. You're the first one involved in this business in a long time. Think of it as an honor."

I think, what the hell, I have a husband probably destroying our marriage in Mexico. I might play that game too. Did he say tribunal? Zaran brings over a matching wrap to cover my dress. Off we go. I am utterly confused (what's new) yet

167

excited. I don't think that he would put me in danger.

We have the Four Seasons "house car." I don't know exactly what model car it is, but it's pretty spectacular. All for four blocks! We enter Per Se and are escorted directly to a private dining room.

What have I gotten myself into now? Within a minute, I see William (who actually looks a lot like Pit Bull, only taller, with his sunglasses on), and a beyond gorgeous, tall, skinny, fit, busty, shiny jet-black hair long enough to hit the seat of a chair when she sits, woman enter together. Fish net stockings, five-inch heels and black leather, of course. Is that the woman I saw in Miami?

It looks like someone like security, maybe a bodyguard, closes the door after them and stays outside of the private room. This creature walks over to Zaran and says, "Ciao baby." She's Italian, and kisses him on both cheeks, then turns and does the same to me. "I am Chelseavonni, and you my dear, may call me Chelseavonni," was she serious or joking? She smirks. Damn, she's funny, too.

"I'm Catie, and you may call me Catie."

"Catie, Catie, Catie," she pronounces three different ways. Shaking her head, she continues, "No, no, no darling, you will be Caterina to me. That is acceptable?" Remembering the words of Zaran, I agree, even though her English is a bit messed up. Hell, it's just a name. I've gone by so many now. Catherine until the end of high school, Catie on that five-day cruise, Cathy starting college, then Cat when Matt changed it as a love name, Mrs. Garcia, Miss Wells before that, Miss Cathy to the kids I care for, and Mom. Now Caterina. Good thing I'm not schizophrenic!

"You certainly have a unique name."

To her reply, "Ohhhhhh," with a sound of disgust in her Italian voice, "My American mother wanted the name Chelsea, and my Italian father wanted an Italian sound to my name. Oh, they heated up this debate. Somehow, they compromised. Something never accomplished together after that incident."

I laugh. "I was named after a soap opera character, Catherine Chancellor. My Mom wanted her daughter to be as strong and powerful as that woman. Mom even went into labor on a Friday morning and refused to go to the hospital until after "The Young and the Restless" aired after lunch. Luck, or strong will, I wasn't born until the next day." I paused and gave a solemn look.

"Caterina, what is on your mind?"

"The woman who played her, Jeanne Cooper, just passed away a few months ago. She, through her character, taught an entire two, maybe three generations, about our opportunities for the empowerment of women. We are stronger because of her actions on the television screen. God rest her soul." Wow, they all bowed their heads. Are they all Catholic? Well, I can see that! At least the Italian and Latino. But Mr. Saudi?

Chelseavonni had the floor. Well, the men actually pulled out our chairs and help seat us. Empowerment for us, yes, but a well-mannered man goes miles. (I do remember how many miles one of these men went with me from years ago!) The three of them have a conversation in Spanish. Then, "Caterina, as you know, we all speak numerous languages. What do you speak?" I simply said sign language. I was serious. I didn't tell them I understood a lot of Spanish, just can't speak it because my high school Spanish teacher was an ass to me in front of my class when I couldn't pronounce the R's correctly, so I gave up speaking. But I know what is said around me. (Oh, that teacher was actually fired because he threw a chair into the wall!) I can keep secrets. Looks like I'll be hearing a lot of secrets tonight.

We had so many courses at dinner. Midway through, the men excused themselves and it was just me and Ms. Gorgeous. She spoke with such authority to these men. I know she's in charge of all of the operations. Whatever that may be. Still not privy to everything.

"First, Caterina, I like your work. And you, of what I know and have found out. How are that husband and assistant doing in Mexico?" How the

HELL did she know about that? "Dear, I do my research before asking someone to join my organization." (Her 'organization." I haven't heard that term since Luke and Laura on General Hospital with Frank Smith in the eighties!). "Zaran and Gear," she begins and I stop her with, "Gear?" "Guillermo...you know Spanish for William." Oh crap, we all have so many names. "They both adore you. They both even had eyes on you since they met you on that cruise. Seems you even fooled them way back then, Miss Seventeen. You're good." Seriously! I've been trying to be a different person from that cruise on. Every day of my life. I even apologize in my sleep to my husband for never being able to tell him this portion, well, 24 hours, I lived. That trashy teen was never to come out again. Prim and proper Catholic girl. Until now.

The boys are back, thirty years later, and I just now realized Gear was the other guy I "dirty danced" with on the cruise. (That term wasn't even around back in 1985!) Funny. Karma's a bitch, as

Angela "exposed" mine. I guess all good things do come to an end. What am I saying?

All of these people must have me confused with someone else. I'm just a Nanny. I just started having adventures for the first time in thirty years. These adventures began this year going down a three-story waterslide with a five-year-old laughing at me while I was holding him going, as I screamed bloody murder. All I've done for these people are photograph some models. I chauffeur kids, change diapers, go fishing, and give lots of love and hugs!

"I like your photographic style. I saw what you did for us this summer. You made us a small fortune. Do you have issues with photographing nudes?" she just stated so matter of fact. I was thinking, sure, up to six months old babies, backside shot. I must have given her a look or some expression with my mouth. She unzipped her leather jacket to reveal the fishnet stockings was actually a bodysuit.

Bless her heart, she was, of course, braless. Seriously people? "What do you think of these?" as she displayed her breasts with pride.

"They are…" what am I supposed to say? "…beautiful." She zipped back up and shook her head, "Exactly. Now you Americans have breast issues. So many breast issues. It's nice to see that toplessness is now acceptable and legal in this city, and of course, South Beach, but really, breastfeeding mothers have hell to pay in most places. You all, meaning Americans, cover them up as if they are taboo. They are just a part of the female body, which is beautiful. Where I come from, it is not an issue on any beach."

I quickly interrupt, "But don't you hate being gawked at?"

"No, my dear. The men can look and have their fantasies. We have the power with these. We can choose to exploit or just be like, yes, they are mine, and you don't have a chance of having them. It's difficult to explain. It's just a way of thinking. Just know that men are weak around these. When we choose to share them, not when we are just with them ourselves. We can get them to do just about anything when they are exposed and suggestively placed at the right time." She motions for more wine and the attendant refills our glasses and leaves. "We raise our males in Europe that the breast is natural. They become accustomed to seeing them in public beaches, on the tube. You Americans have them in magazines hidden behind gas station counters. I believe women who use their bodies, like dancers, you call them strippers, are really the intelligent ones. Some even use that income to buy higher education. Most women, especially the marrieds, use their sexuality on their husbands. How many times have you gone down, for other reasons than just to please your man? Plus, sex should be fun and natural. Enjoyable, unless pain is part of one's enjoyment. So darling, back to my question. Will you photograph some women for me? We are branding a new market, called 'Harems'. I will explain more after tonight. Also, let us do a day at the spa next week. We will cut and color you, polish your nails, fix the eyebrows, and get massages before heading to a glorious mud bath." I laugh inside. The last mud bath I took was by accident when I slipped in the Cary, North Carolina, pond trying to catch frogs with the little boys!

"You don't like how I look?" as she smirks and puts her finger to her mouth before continuing.

"Let's just get you to sparkle. I'll set it up in Milan next weekend. There you can learn more about this endeavor, and practice your empowerment. The body's a beautiful thing." Ugh, that's a Matt expression.

Well, there's a European female's point to view. Shopping in Milan?!? I was beginning to wonder where Zaran was hiding, as I am locked up with this Amazon Goddess obsessed with boobs and my looks.

She continues, "After hearing about you all year, I still don't get what Zaran sees in you. Yes, I see that homey kind of beauty. You know Gear took a stabbing because of you." I am so lost. "I have heard this story that after your night together with Zaran all those moons ago, Gear came to his cabin door to straighten him out. You know, you were supposed to end up being one of their working girls, and Zaran would not have it. After lengthy discussions and shouting matches, both men left the cruise and Zaran stabbed Gears' side as he entered his black Datsun 280Z. Nobody knew it was Zaran, even as the stabbing made the news. It took these men years to be best friends again."

I interrupt, "Friends?"

"Yes, they were in boarding school and undergrad together. They were like brothers, and more so now since Mehmet's death. He never told you? You didn't know that after you didn't meet him on your birthday, he went to finish his last years before taking his bar exams. He just studied, studied, studied. No life but books. He looked you up when he was done, all to find out that you had married and were with child. And you kept having children. He vowed to find you after the last child left for college. So, the hunt began and with the power of the internet, it took no time at all. We tried through the years to find him love, and we matched him with other such beautiful women. All he did was work. Last September, he told us it was time. That's when I heard the story. He always gets what he wants. He gave you that time with your children. Now he wants the rest of your time. He'll give you anything. He even bought and decorated for you a fortress on Lake Como. Over twenty years ago it's been for you. Something about viewing the Alps. You'll have it after we meet in Milan for business. It's time to rebrand."

And then, Zaran and William, I mean Gear, walk back in. The waiter starts to serve us more food. I've never had so many courses. Plus, was that story real? Should I be flattered, or is he a psychotic stalker? Lifetime movie in the making? Can you tell I watch too much television?

As the men return, I just remembered that my passport has expired. William tells me he will take care of it and have one ready before Milan. How did he know I was going to Milan? He will also need a picture of me. These people have their ways. Is that good? Have I decided to join them? What about my life here? I'm just a middle-aged nanny!

Chelseavonni remarks in Spanish to the men, "Haz lo que sea necesario. La quiero en el negocio. Zar, puedes tenerla para," meaning, "Do whatever it takes. I want her in the business. Zar, you can have her for," and I didn't comprehend the rest of the Spanish. I acted like I didn't understand any of their conversation. Before dessert is served, both William and Chelseavonni make an exit.

Zaran and I are alone. He dims the lights. How I pray he doesn't want to have sex here, right on the table. All I can think about is one of the last "Devious Maids" episodes where they do it on the kitchen counter...and all that cleaning/sanitizing after. But this is a public place. He's no "domineering Mr. Grey" from that book, either. What is he? Oh, I do remember. There are no words in the English dictionary to describe Zaran in bed.

He just touches my hand at the table. I still get shivers when he does this. "What do you want from me?"

He leans over to start to kiss me, stops and whispers, "Exactly what I told you on the cruise. A lifetime of adventure. We can start that lifetime now." He puts his hand around my neck, ever so gently, but firmly. His face gets so close to mine. He then gently touches my lips and I tremble. Lips lock smoothly. Tongues collide and then his tongue touches every tooth in my mouth, in a slow, wet, hot, sweeping motion. He has taken my breath away. Okay, we are officially intimate.

We stop. He hands me another gift. I open it. It's a watch. A very fancy and expensive watch. It even has diamonds on it. I don't know watch brands, as I only use my iPhone clock on the home screen. "To replace your Swatch," he says. The back is engraved May 22, 1985. Zaran puts the watch on my left wrist and we both notice my wedding rings. No comments.

SHOELESS

He wants to go out dancing, but I decline. I can't remember the last time I went dancing. Maybe my sister's wedding a decade ago? Before I know it, we are headed back to room 3207 in the Upper Tower. I'm so confused. Catie from the cruise is coming back stronger than ever. But what am I doing? Thoughts of my husband come racing through me. I love him, but what I saw and heard are no match for ever saving a marriage, or is there hope with Matt?

SHOELESS

"So tonight, kiss me like it's do or die,
And take me to the other side."
-Jason Derulo, The Other Side

I had almost two glasses of Merlot at dinner, which really helped my cough that's now back again with a vengeance. It comes and goes, but when it's here, watch out. We start out on the terrace with the gorgeous view. It's getting breezy up here, so before we head inside, I get closer to Zaran. The chemistry is unbelievable. Just like thirty years ago. Zaran pulls me tight to his chest; arms wrapped around me, and kisses me. A long soft kiss, then hard with tongues and teeth clashing again. I don't recall this kind of kiss with Matt. Why am I even thinking of Matt right now? Catholic guilt, Catholic guilt, Catholic guilt. I start to walk inside and he pulls the sheer floral-patterned fabric off of my dress. Just as he is about to let go of it and let it fly in the wind, I catch it. "It's too beautiful to lose," I say and don't put it back my chest. There I stand, fully exposed. Bigger than thirty years ago, due to four pregnancies, and a bit fuller and heavier, yet droopier. But I'm keeping my self-confidence up. Am I actually doing this?

He says, "No, Catie, you are beautiful, not that piece of material." We walk to his room and lay on his bed. He removes his coat, tie and shirt. He is muscular and ever so fit for being about sixty. His mouth goes straight to my breasts. Licking around my areolas, then sucking and biting my nipples just enough to feel it down below. I roll over on top of him. I feel the same passion as when I was seventeen with him. Our one incredible, long night together. After I kiss his lips, I then put my nipple in his mouth. Oh, I can feel that below. Then my other nipple. He grabs both and proceeds to suck them both simultaneously! That would not have been possible in my teenage years. Larger breasts have some benefits. I turn around and pull my dress up so that I can sit on top of him, to want to unzip him, and arch my back so my hair can touch his chest. At least I have some black lacey panties on! As he lies on his back, he grabs by breasts. I then begin by removing his belt and unbuttoning his slacks. I can see what is happening to him. I haven't even touched him down there yet! Then my coughing begins. And it doesn't want to stop. He moves me off of him and helps me up and gets me some water. He leaves his bedroom and returns with another box for me. That gorgeous coral lingerie.

I excuse myself to "my" bathroom and look at myself. What am I doing? Do I really want this? Believe it or not, I say a quick prayer for guidance. Weird time to pray, I know. I get out of the blue dress and slip on the coral nightie. It's chiffon, and falls straight to the ground. It's something you'd see in the old-time movies. A light knock at the door, and Zaran enters this magnificent bathroom. I am facing the mirror, oh no, my favorite place to have sex, and he licks my neck! Licks my earlobes, and removes my hairpins. My long wavy hair is all over. "Catie, you are so beautiful my darling." How I love that word! As he is still in back of me, I can see everything in the mirror. This is so hot. His huge hands go under the chiffon on my sides and he is feeling my breasts. He then takes his hands and drops the sides of this gown exposing all my top area. He is watching in the mirror. He kneads my breasts, massages my shoulders, starts to pull down my nightgown and then the cough from hell begins again. Still topless now, I go to the kitchen with him to get a stronger drink. The coughing doesn't seem to want to stop.

At this moment, his cell phone rings. He looks down at the number. "I have to get this my darling" and he walks to his room. I pull the sides of my nightie back up. I hear him speaking another language, not Spanish or Italian.

After a few minutes, Zaran comes out of his room with a small suitcase. "My darling," as he removes my top again, and caresses each breast, "Expose them all you want here. They are beautiful." He gently kisses my lips with his tongue again. "I must leave you now, for just a short time, as my client needs me in Saudi Arabia immediately. I am sorry, but I must go. The flight is now, with a plane waiting. Please understand, you can stay as long as you want. The butler is on call. I don't know how long I'll be. May I see your phone?" I pull it from my purse; he changes out the SIM card. I don't know why. "Keep this on you at all times. It will work internationally. I will meet you in Milan at the end of the week and then I have a surprise for you on Lake Como! I want to be your man. I'm going to be your man." Sure, an invisible man tonight.

"I have to leave on my flight tomorrow. I finally have my tests and doctor's appointment on Monday. There are some things about my health I haven't told you. We'll discuss it next time." Oh wait, maybe the appointment is next week. I'm confused. With that, he kissed me like never before. I love how he kisses. As he leaves, and I can't help thinking, was this sign from God? Thankfully, this man, from what I remember, is not into quickies.

Hey, he left me just like he did thirty years ago. Then it was in a cruise cabin, now a suite that would cost me half a year's salary per night.

Because this is not his real residence, he doesn't have personal things around. But knowing what little I do know of him, I decide not to go many through what is left of his things. He probably has cameras in here. I go back to my room, water in hand, and look at myself in the mirror. I pull down my top and really look at myself. Not too bad for a 46-year-old mother of four young adults.

I go to the bedroom balcony, and expose myself to Central Park in the dark. It is a feeling of freedom. Who knows, maybe I can do this someday in the daylight, laying down below in Central Park, reading a book with the other women.

But as I'm outside on the balcony, baring not only my breasts in the moonlight, something is happening in my soul. I've been searching for various answers. Oh my God!

SHOELESS

My mind is full of thoughts, but now I remember that I never called my YouTube friend Dy. She is "The Sexiest Couponing Queen" who lives in a one-bedroom apartment in Brooklyn, with her little girls. I guess I really can't tell her that I'm in New York City, but I do know that if I ever need a place to hide, she has a wall of toilet paper and paper towels! Who would look there?

SHOELESS

"I have finally seen the light.
I have finally realized what you mean..."
-Muse, <u>Madness</u>

After an entire night of peaceful sleep, in a bed that felt like clouds, I woke up abruptly early in the morning after having the strangest of dreams. It's dawn and I walk back out to the balcony. As I look across Central Park, watching the joggers and cleaning crew, the size of ants, something hits me. My dreams were real. Flashbacks of the last few months. Images of the teenager I saw on my Facebook account while in Washington; the tween on the news in Atlanta; the girl on the top back page of the Sunday Red Plum coupon insert about Missing Children; and The Wal-Mart images of

Missing and Exploited Children. Each time I felt a connection to them, at first because I thought I was just sad because I am a mom and these were somebody's little lovies. But no! I think I photographed each one of them. Here in New York, a few months ago. But how can that be? These little gifts from God are from all over the country. Why would they be my models for this man's agency, or was what was William really using them for? I am so stunned, almost paralyzed. Could I be involved with these missing children?

I quickly gather my things, take the limo to the airport several hours early, with a quick stop at CVS to buy a notebook with my soon-to-be-expiring ECBs. After passing security, I start to write down all I can remember since meeting these men. So, from about the end of March until now, the middle of August. This notebook that you are reading. I used to think I had a wild imagination. Years of being brainwashed I suppose. Or watching too many Lifetime movies. You, of the FBI, can decide. But this really happened to me.

SHOELESS

My flight is delayed by several hours. I start to get paranoid. I continue writing, get some lunch, and use the ladies' room. It seems this lady keeps looking over at me. Now I know I am paranoid. As I board, I am told that they changed my seat assignment. I feel squashed in the farthest row you can get, and the corner seat too. That lady from the bathroom sits one row up, on the opposite aisle. Luckily, the man next to me, wearing a cell phone company logoed golf shirt, looks harmless as he plays useless video games on his phone. Doesn't anyone read a real book anymore on an airplane?

Because of arriving several hours early to the airport, along with the delay, I am able to get as much of this story out to you. As you do a background check on me, you will see that I am not a criminal, have never been to jail, had only one traffic violation many years ago, and am not under any psychiatric care. Except for owing the IRS, I am pretty squeaky clean. You can't even fill a kill folder on me. Boring life. Until Zaran showed up. This nanny now has had magnificent adventures.

Side note:

I have the flash drive in my possession. You can figure out who I am by my seat number, 32A. Lousy window seat, as all I see is the engine when I look outside.

As I am the last person off of this flight, the flight attendant says, "Thanks for flying with us, have a nice day…"

I smile back at her, look her straight in the eyes and say, "Thanks. I left a spiral notebook in the front pocket of my seat, 32A. Please get it to a TSA agent immediately."

"The struggles I'm facing
The chances I'm taking
Sometimes might knock me down but
No, I'm not breaking..."
-Miley Cyrus, The Climb

This has been the first time I have really chronicled, or preserved, the details of my life, since the one and only journal I kept for all of 1985. I used to call these "diaries." Now, I think I will try again writing my life events. This time I will call it a "journal." So, here it goes.

Saturday, August 17, 2013

I go home to find another box, filled with money, on the back porch. More money, but I didn't do any actual work this time. There was also a key. Fancier than my own keys.

I rush to Mass and we have a visiting priest. He's actually a Cardinal. He talks about the new Pope and how we all have to set a fire. Not a literal fire, another kind of fire. He will also be speaking tomorrow afternoon about various things. I might go. Instead of rushing out before Mass has ended, which our Pastor has verbally scorned us for, I wait for the Cardinal to proceed down the aisle. He gives a hand gestured blessing. The good Lord knows that I need it now more than ever. I even wait in another line to thank him for his words and I receive a handshake. This is the closest I've ever been to a Cardinal! As I am getting to the parking lot, a friend of Matt and mine comes up and says "Hey, beautiful!" Okay, we've been friends for over a dozen years, and this is the first time he, or anyone has called me that. Except Zaran. Happy coincidence or should that be code from Zaran? I'm going home.

SHOELESS

At home and for the first time in years, I set the alarm on the house. I watch the premiere of Lifetimes *Baby Sellers*. Wow! They do make movies about regular people. I'm a regular person, now with a tweak. Not twerk, tweak! By the end of the movie, I realize that I should have sent my notebook to the ICE agents, not FBI. They probably didn't get it anyway.

I can't sleep. I cough all night. My mind is racing.

How do I fill this Sunday? I try to pray. I try to keep busy. I go down to the mailbox to collect this past week's mail. A booklet from an Alaskan cruise line. Seriously? Oh yeah, I ordered it when it was posted on the coupon forum. Maybe I'll get back on the coupon site.

After picking up the cruise brochure, I decide no more cruises in my lifetime!

I sit and watch Oprah's "Super Soul Sunday." Oops! I've got to do my 21 Day Meditation. I am not myself. I even skip getting my multiple copies of the Sunday newspaper for the coupons. This is happening more frequently. I need to file these!

Remembering that our church is sponsoring a talk from the visiting Cardinal, I gussy up and go. If there is a hit on me (just kidding) they can do me in at church. I know I have a wild imagination again. But that notebook could be been in the wrong hands. Or maybe the cleaning crew onboard just dumped it, before the flight attendant could retrieve it, or … enough. If the FBI did receive the notebook, I should be seeing them soon. Yeah, right. They probably think I'm just a bored housewife with crazy thoughts.

Still having a few hours until Church, I go to see the movie, "The Butler." It was amazing! Everyone deserves an Oscar, not just for their exquisite and fine acting talents, but for educating all of us about the Civil Rights movement. Our history classes in my high school days did an awful job at accomplishing this task.

I did have an incident, though, at the movie. The couple a few seats down would not get off of their cell phones. The phones were lighting up throughout the movie. Texting incessantly. I finally politely asked them to stop. They told me to move my seat. Really? Then they flashed both of their phones' flashlights on me. Sure, at any movie this can happen, but this movie? I left the movie and was about to get in my car when a couple kept looking at the ground. When I asked, they said her Pandora bracelet had opened and her charms were scattered. Being a Pandora owner myself, I helped them locate some of the charms. As I get back in the car, I remember Matt and all of his Pandora gifts to me. Will he ever call me back? I highly doubt it.

I try and organize the stuff in my house. The kids left to go to college while I was in Texas. I am in a quiet and empty house.

I haven't heard a word from Matt. It's Sunday, our official Skype day. I will try and keep busy. I look at my "to-do-lists." I really should start to remove the caulk in the shower. Forget it, I'll do it tomorrow. I must look up information on human trafficking. I head downstairs. As I turn on my laptop, my cell rings. Could it be my husband? No, wrong ringtone. It's the other cell! Zaran!

"Catie, I want to apologize," he begins with his distinctive accent. "I am in Saudi Arabia helping a client and want you near me. I can meet you in Milan tomorrow evening. I've sent a car out front of your home and all I need is for you to walk out of your door right now and enter it. No packing required." What am I supposed to say to that? "We will meet the organization there and then I will take you to the villa that I have for us. That is the key in your box I left you."

"Seriously? I can, but I must be back in a week, as I have important medical lab exams that I have to complete. I need to tell you about my health." I am breathing better since I picked up the new inhaler. I don't start back to work until the end of next week, so technically, I can travel. My college kids don't check in too much, and I have no idea where Matt is located. This time away could help the FBI if they want to follow up on my notebook.

Monday, August 26, 2013

I don't think this journaling thing is going to work. I haven't written in a week. I was a little busy. That's an understatement. I actually didn't get home until after midnight last night. A week I will never forget. I hope that it can help others. There is still no sign of my husband. After my last week, I don't care anymore. Well, maybe a little.

So, I will start the day with my 21 Day Daily Meditation from Oprah and Deepak. I actually didn't meditate at all last week, as I was "away." Plus, the program "officially ended" yesterday, but I still have all of their emails. Maybe meditating will clear my head. Shower and change and off I go. I don't know why, but am still paranoid about everything. I actually look under the car to see if any bombs are underneath. Like I'd know what that would look like, but remember the first episode of Miami Vice back in the 80's and how the car exploded with his partner in it! (Why do I recall these facts? I need a good therapist!) As I drive down the cul-de-sac, I wave good morning to my neighbor and she gives me a look. Yes, I know my yard needs work. It's hard being neighbors with people in this subdivision as they are members of the garden club and architectural committees. I told them I like the wild look. (The homeowners association didn't find that excuse funny and said we had to cut our grass and fix the broken tree or we would be fined!)

As I leave the block, a white cargo van veers in front me. Geez, there are a lot of trucks in the neighborhood today. There's now another one in back of me. Cable television van? Sewer van? Whatever! I see a plane fly overhead. For a woman that hasn't traveled much before this nanny job, I sure am racking up the bonus miles! Even if some trips were never known to my family.

Off to the hospital for my chest x-ray and pulmonary function tests. How I want to breathe without coughing and sounding like I'm dying all of the time. As I head off of Exit 7, Leesville Road, onto 540, I think about how I hate, and I don't use that word lightly, how the traffic will be cluttered later at rush hour. Every car will be stopped across the way because someone decided to bottleneck drivers into three lanes, instead of just keeping that lane long. Okay, ADHD again. Someone lets me merge onto the road and I give *The Thank You Wave*. I don't think the Southern Newbies here know what that is. Bless their hearts!

I put on G105 and remember that I get to go to the "Listeners Lounge" with the Backstreet Boys tomorrow night. No! That was for last week. I forgot! (I was busy elsewhere in this world!) Oh, I need to call Char later and see if she wants to have lunch this week. Something to look forward to, as our last lunch was eventful in my life! I get onto I-40 and see that van is still in back of me. Coincidence, I know. I started watching too much television when Matt started traveling. I am listening to Bob, Erica, Peanut Butter and Elic on the radio to distract me. I change lanes, just for the hell of it, and that van is back on my ass. So, I change again, and it follows. Seriously coincidental? Now I'm in Durham County, I wonder if I should get in the far-right lane that is now reserved for "Buses on Shoulders." Perhaps the traffic video cameras can catch my illegal move and a cop will stop me. No, then all I'll get is a ticket for who would believe that I am being followed? Too cheap to take a chance.

I come up to my Exit 273A for the hospital. With thinking of that stupid van on my rear, and Triangle Transit Bus Route #800 slowing down, I am unable to merge and miss the exit. Seriously? Now I am laughing too much on what Bob and the Showgram are saying and I miss the 15-501 exit. Erica says something about "Out of sight, out of mind…" and I think of Matt. SO TRUE!!! Where is my head? Okay, as I'm driving, I know that Char lives out here, but is at work so I won't call her. I think I can make it back to 15-501 from the next exit. I think. Forget using my cell phone for directions. I am woman! Hear me roar!

SHOELESS

Okay, I'm now in Orange County and the road diverges into two lanes. As I look into my rearview mirror, I see another white cargo van in back of me. What?!? The two-mile sign then the one-mile sign. This is no coincidence. Think! I drive up the #266 exit and stay in the middle lane. Stop light changes to red! Time for guts! One of the vans is now next to me in the left lane, and the other in back of me. I'm directly in back of the median that separates going either right or left. I can see a semi-truck coming up the ramp. The light changes and I push down on the gas pedal and swerve up and over the median and head right with a semi honking like hell at me! What a rush, I could have been killed! But I don't see either van and I take the first right at the stoplight. Still don't see the van, but, crap, workmen are paving the road! I am stopped. Still shaking, but stopped! I follow the "pilot car" down Whitfield Road, and as I do, a giant bird, was that an eagle, flies over my car. This is such a strange day. So, I get to Erwin and take a right. Now I'm trying to remember what the road is that connects down to

15-501. I see the Mt. Moriah Road sign, facing the wrong direction, and take it. Somehow, I follow it to the road, turn right on 15-501 and take it all the way in to the hospital. I figure, if the vans were really after me, they will find me soon. But who are they? Zaran's team? Security? Are they trying to kill me because they got a hold of my confessional notebook before the FBI? Or am I wanted by the FBI because of last week?

After entering the hospital, quickly, I first go for my chest x-ray. My blood pressure is sky high! Funny how when you're in that little room, you can even fluster a stranger. As I put my bag down, the technician says he will close the blinds and hands me a blue top like paper cover for me to wear. I'm thinking, what the hell. I give it back to him, and take off my top and bra right in front of him. Poor guy turned beet red! He is puzzled, even as a medical professional, and tries to tell me something about having to wear the wrinkled sheet. I'm thinking, the hell with modesty, as soon as I raise my arms for the x-ray, he'll have a side view anyways. How'd I get so bold?

I go up to another floor and meet the next technician. Funny, he has the same last name as me! Tech Garcia does the spirometry and a diffusion test. He explains that if I get dizzy, he will catch me. I joke that I might tip him over, as he is a lot smaller than me. I start to blow in the carbon monoxide, nitrogen, methane, and I start to feel dizzy. My head feels...

SHOELESS

"My songs know what you did in the dark..."
-Fall Out Boy, <u>My Songs Know What You Did</u>
<u>*in The Dark (Light 'em Up)*</u>

I wake up in a hospital room connected to tubes and machines. THIS DAMN LUPUS.

Two people in suits are standing in the corner. I recognize the man. He was the cell phone company guy sitting next to me on the airplane. Was the woman driving one of the vans that were chasing me?

The man says, "I'm ICE special agent Wayne Brody and this is my partner," he said her name but I am too out of it to pay attention. Yes, that was the lady I saw in the bathroom at the airport, and again on my flight. "We read your notebook. Thank you."

What is going on? "Are you strong enough to answer some questions?" The nurse leaves the room. There is a guard outside of my door. Why?

I scooch up in the bed and begin. "Thank you for coming. It's been a strange five months, of not understanding. Maybe it's nothing. Maybe I just have an over active imagination. But you read what I wrote, and you're here. So, I guess it's something. It wasn't until Mass a few weeks ago when Fr. Bob said in his homily about not being a bystander to bullies. I think this is even worse. I got so caught up in all of the money… all to pay back all of my IRS debts. We never seem to get ahead, and then this happened." My cough from hell begins again. I take a drink as the woman hands me a glass. .

She confidently states, "You're going to be alright. Really, you are. We have a lot of questions and not enough time. We need to start."

I listen. "Do you or did you ever know a Guillermo Gonzalez on a cruise in 1985?"

I tell them no. "I only remember the dirty dancing with Liam." She shows me a photograph of a man. Do you recognize this man (showing me a picture of someone in his later sixties) "Yes, that's William Gonzalez."

Then she shows me a picture of Liam, way back when. I recognize him right away. "That's Liam." Why do you have his mug shot? They explain that this is William Gonzalez, the man in the current image. Back then he was one of the cocaine cowboys/kingpins smuggling cocaine by air to Parkland, Florida and living near you in Boca Raton. He went by various names back then. He was the man I danced with then and have been working for now. I never met him after that night.

"Can you tell us what happened after you got to Hazar's room the night before you left the cruise ship so long ago? You stopped journaling thoughts here." I hadn't heard Zaran being called Hazar since the day I met him all of those years ago. Wasn't it bad enough that I finally released my pandora's box of dirty little secrets to them? Them, the ICE agents. I remember every little sordid detail. But this one is going to my grave.

After I danced with Liam, Zaran gestured to me to come to see him at the door. He publicly put his hand around the side of my dress. Kissing me intently, we walked over to his cabin. It was nothing like the dorm room style closet of a room I was staying in. This was a suite. Like the ones on the Love Boat television show. You could walk around and it had a deck outside. He told me that if I entered this room, I would be his forever. I thought it was a line. I hesitantly walked into his room and he shut the door, he opened a bottle of something. I only had a few sips and we just started kissing...

A few hours went by and we were lying in bed. A knock was at the door. Please don't let it be my aunts! Zaran got up, completely nude and answers the door. He was one solidly built man. And he was like the Energizer Bunny! I can't believe I did all of what I just did.

"I'm sorry, but even on my deathbed, I can't give you the details. Isn't it enough to know that we had sex?" All night long, until a knock on the door.

He answered it; I didn't see or know who he was talking to. He put on his clothes, kissed my forehead, and said he'd see me soon. He left and I decided to get up and return to my little box of a cabin. It was almost five in the morning and I had to get ready for the hell I would receive from my aunts. But they weren't even back in the room yet. I vowed no one would know what took place in the Bahamas and on that ship. Funny, how ICE is my "No one."

"Wait until this story comes out as a Lifetime or Oprah Movie of the week, then you can see my character nude on screen, almost thirty years ago. Trust me, the girls were a lot more perky then." (We didn't have words like "the girls" back then!) The female laughs, the old guy doesn't get it. They bring out a folder. "Mrs. Garcia, you are right about your 'kill folder.' We had you as a person of interest back in 1985." They show me another photograph. Only this time it is of Zaran and I walking on the beach, holding hands, in the Bahamas, back in 1985. The one place I thought cameras were not going to capture little ole me. Let alone an 8x10 three decades later. Well, the government has a glossy of me topless. I sure don't look that way anymore! Whatever. What a long-distance lens they must have used for me not to notice. "Can you verify who this is in the photograph?" says the man, staring at a topless me long ago.

"Yes sir, it's me, and Zaran, that's who you call Hazar. Long story, comic book thing." He whips out another photo, this time taken a few nights ago when we were walking in together at Per Se in NYC. Again, I stated it was the two of us. Then he showed me a photo of me alone on the balcony, in the moonlight, over thirty floors high. Seriously?!? Well, at least I can see that my breasts don't look too bad nowadays.

The agent continues, "All we could dig up on you was your family portrait. Plus, some press clippings of you and your photography studio awards. Oh, and press releases of you and a 'Jefferson Decker'."

I quickly interrupt with, "He's just a fellow colleague…when I had my studio." (I didn't say that he was also a hunk of an African-American man). I had to change the topic because that last topic could be a whole other notebook. So, I went with, "How long have you been following me?"

"The government has been watching Hazar, or, Zaran, since he came over from Saudi Arabia in the eighties. We weren't on the cruise, except the private island, so we didn't know the extent of your relationship until recently. You were dropped to just a "person of interest" when we found out you were a minor and just went about your life. I doubt he knew your real age. Do you know he is twelve years older than you? Even back then?" Wow, that explains a lot! I interrupt, telling them everything I did was consensual and no drugs were used. Well, except alcohol, but I never drank too much.

"He was into drug distribution, and prostitution, as was Liam and they had a falling out. Here, watch." They turned on their iPad and showed the 6:00 news of the night with Dwight

Lauderdale and Anne Bishop from Channel 11, Miami, (then known as 'Dead County') in 1985: "Drug King Pin, Guillermo Gonzalez, also known as GG, was stabbed while leaving a cruise ship Saturday at the docks in Miami. His whereabouts are currently unknown and no suspects have been apprehended. We are told by a source that he will survive."

The agent continues, "Catherine, is that your name you now use?" I nod my head. "GG is the man in this picture (showing me the mug shot of Liam again). Guillermo is Spanish for William, and Liam is a nickname he used. See, the last four letters in the name William. Today, both of these high-powered untouchable men are involved in the lucrative world of human trafficking. Not just the bunches of little ones found all bundled under a house in other countries along with ours. I think you know where I'm going with this. This is high end."

Well, it wasn't until the restaurant that I figured out they knew each other then but human trafficking? How?

"Wait. But how did you find me with Zaran over the last few months?" Then I ask, "Am I in trouble?"

"Catherine, we weren't following you to hurt you. We were protecting you. That pat down from the TSA in Naples was just to bug your stuff and phone. Remember those surveillance cameras in the Naples house? We were making sure you were safe. We intercepted their regular security to also know how you were. You are busy with four little boys! We were exhausted watching you do just the daily work. When we found out Zaran was in Naples at the same time as you, since the airline passenger manifesto with your name on it raised a red flag that the two of you were in the same vicinity. He was actually on that little canal sightseeing boat. He was following you. We think he photographed you while you were in the pool with the little boys. You've got to careful what you post on Facebook!" (All I did was showing myself alone outside standing by the pool!) "We also watched you by having an agent at the loud Cadillac in Seattle. Then, all the way to the flight from Texas, to when you then left for New York City. That new delayed flight was to get our team together for you. And the van this morning. How did you learn those driving moves?"

"Easy. I learned a lifetime supply of safety from the Oprah Winfrey Show, from many years ago. If you think you are being followed, drive to a police station. I didn't know of any around here. Well, once I lost the van, I came back here for my appointment. I was determined never to get caught, because Oprah taught the world to never be taken to a second location. And if you are ever placed in a trunk, to kick out the taillight and wave like crazy. I can even tell you what to do if a bear comes after you!" My cough returns. Harder this time. I'm beyond shocked!

I think a little more. My crazy imagination was a reality! "Oh my God, I was right. I did recognize those girls from Atlanta, Seattle, and the mountains. I photographed them! In New York. But how? How is this human trafficking? I do remember the girls on the billboard, the one on the Red Plum coupons ad on top of the page, the Facebook search, and the flyer in The Wal-Mart. How did they go from being models for me to trafficked?"

The agents started to explain that this trio, including Chelseavonni, the ring leader, may have been involved in the July 29 *Operation Cross Country*, where ICE recovered 105 teens in 76 cities. However, they were cleared. But the agents think the teens they trafficked were for international sex selling and commercial exploitation. Then they said I was protected every minute over the last months, including extra eyes where I worked. "Did you really think the gardeners and cleaning staff had that much to do?" The only time they thought I was in danger was in the private dining room at Per Se because they saw Chelseavonni enter with William. "She is a very international and elusive bitch. The highest on their food chain." Wayne asked, "What did the two of you talk about when you were alone with her?" I told them breasts and he said we'd have a deeper discussion about the private dining room at another time. Like what am I supposed to say, she's got a great rack? Whatever!

I was feeling exhausted again. My head needed a break but they told me not to sleep because the drugs they gave me in the pulmonary function test should be out of my system soon. And the technician had added something to stop the horrible cough completely.

I was afraid to ask but I did, "If you saw everything, did that include room 3207? Can you do that?" Of course, they can, they are the FBI, rather ICE.

"Yes, nice dress," said the agent and she smiled.

"We have disconnected the surveillances and are redecorating this room for future guests!" I really thought I looked for cameras in the bathroom. I need a refresher lesson on what exactly to search for!

SHOELESS

"…or you can start speaking up…
Say what you want to say, and let the words fall
out…
-Sara Bareilles, Brave

I was awoken soon by the agents. "I'm sorry; how long was I out?" They explained that it was for just a few minutes, but somehow reassured me that I was going to be fine. How did they know? Fine as in physically from health problems, or physically from harm, or mentally, because this is so surreal. I am just an average everyday nanny.

So, we continued. They explained how the girls had   arrived in New York. Some were runaways and others wanted to make it big on Broadway.

"We are still trying to fill in the details, that's why we are here. With your help they can figure out more of these cases," said the female agent.

"But won't I be in danger if I help you? They will know these details came from me."

"We know. We have a guard right outside your door. We want to offer you a special witness protection program with relocating and a new identity. And to work with us." He paused, "But you have to 'die' first." He put up air quotes. "Not literally, but we have set up your death if you want your family safe."

Lord, am I confused? "What? Aren't I already dying here today? That's why I…"

She interrupted and said, "We set up your pulmonary function test to have you end up here. They added an extra chemical for you to pass out, hence the death bed stage. Your kidneys are not in that bad of a shape that your docs had previously told you. But to the world, you will have multiple organ failure and cardiac arrest, caused by your

219

lupus and the test. Yes, we know all about your health history." Of course, they do. "Also, we need the details of what happened last week. After New York City." That is when I knew I must help them. I learned so much on last week's trip to Milan and Lake Como. I couldn't put this information in writing.

This is beyond words. In all of the television and movies that I've seen, I never would have thought this was possible. Save my family? Save those girls? But I'd lose my life. My real life. Plus, the true "Love of My Life." He has my heart, and I his. Even after all of this mess. I'd be losing everything. Even my couponing family on YouTube. I just hit 8,500 views! Oh, and the precious family that I work for! Those four little souls! What will they tell them? Who will care for them? I've been told that it's not easy finding a great nanny.

"Catherine, we need you to decide now. There's no time. We know you were on a private jet with him last week. But we have no details as to your whereabouts last week. You know that if you follow Zaran's life, you will be dead sooner than later. Zaran won't kill you. He's wanted you for decades. You'll be a target, be it for various reasons, even by his enemies. If you stay alive, you could be recognized by many of his enemies, and the dead end would be the easiest part of their terror. Honestly, consider the last thirty years of your life as a gift. Who knows what would have become of you if you were with Zaran immediately after the cruise?"

Crap, it just hit me, that news channel from Miami in 1985 was about the stabbing of Zaran hurting William, (then called Liam). Ooh, I can't keep everybody's names straight, and it was about me! Chelseavonni heard the story correctly! Liam wanted to sell me back then and for some reason, Zaran wanted me. All to himself. Forever. And his "forever" is beginning again in his mind. Now I know there's no way out of this mess! I drift off.

"I used to bite my tongue and hold my breath…"
-Katy Perry, <u>Roar</u>

"**W**here's my husband? What will he know? And my kids?"

"Matt is now being detained in a Mexican prison trying to get here to you. He has been alerted to your impending death, and as a PA he understands the urgency of your multiple organ failure. Unfortunately, his name, Matthew Garcia, matches another Matthew Garcia, wanted for murder in Mexico. He will be treated fairly." Darn, I think, can I ask for a version of waterboarding?

222

SHOELESS

Okay, maybe not that extreme, but I wish we could have finished the mess we left. I still love him and the almost thirty years together. Does he feel any guilt? I'm starting to feel some about last week. Or was Angela part of Zaran's plot to get me? I don't know.

Wayne continues, "Your husband is currently under our protection, but will not be able to be here for a few weeks. All of your kids are now headed to Mexico to try and help him. They will hear of your death when they are in Mexico. Your "body" will be accidently cremated before your husband or the kids get back to North Carolina. We have to begin now. What do you want to do?" Great, do I die this second?

"We will see you later tonight in the back of the hospital. The transport team will take you downstairs after it gets dark. Take the right door to the outside. All you will have are the clothes you came here with this morning. We will provide the rest. Are you willing to "die" to save all of these

223

lives?" This is beyond anything my imagination could have created.

Then they started to explain what happened to the photographs I took in New York City. Modeling my ass! They took the photos that I made and had them on a secure site, on the "Dark Web," where people "purchased" the girls for an obscene amount of money. Some had already become sex slaves all over the world.

The agent pulls out another large envelope with a single photo in it. I look at four preteens all with happy faces and arms around each other. It is signed, *"THANK YOU CATHERINE!"* Agent Wayne says, "These are the girls you saved from the Louisiana tip you gave me. Yes, that police officer in Louisiana was me." I don't understand and say, "I thought I saw only two girls?"

He replies, "You saw two, but there were two more still in the van. You did the right thing letting us know about the girls. We wish more people would speak up." It's been decided.

I show them my purse with the keychain inside of it. "The flash drive is hidden in the attached lipstick shaped piece here, along with the cell phone that Zaran gave me."

Then the agents also told me they found my one and only real diary from 1985, the second half of my senior year of high school to the end of my first semester of college. I didn't include the Catie Cruise, only the Catherine Cruise, to the Bahamas.

The Cardinal's words came to me. I will start a fire!

This is so hard. No, that's an understatement. It's almost impossible. But this is what I did to save my family and those children that I photographed, along with other children being human trafficked.

I was getting ready to leave, with my size STRONG jeans on, having officially lost 30 pounds at my weigh-in this morning at the hospital, I noticed something in my back pocket. It was the little pocket edition of the Living Faith from the

Seattle trip, that I forgot to give to Charlotte. No more having a best friend! I opened it to today's date. Finding and following Jesus.

As I had a few quiet moments to reflect upon my decision, I prayed like never before. I am scared. I am doing the right thing. I can't imagine the depths of pain that the many girls, and boys, along with their families, are feeling.

I have found my voice. My purpose! I am determined to make a difference.

There's a knock on my door. It's past supper time, but I am too nervous to eat. I get up from the hospital bed and am moved by wheelchair on the elevator to the basement floor. The hallway is white, sterile, and long. You could hear the echoes of a pin drop, if there were noise. We are all alone as we pass the morgue doors. The person that is pushing me stops in front of the doors and tells me it's time to get up and walk the rest of the hall to the back doors. As I stand, a little groggy from the meds earlier today, the person disappears with my wheelchair.

SHOELESS

I am now all alone on this perplexing journey. It is such a combination of now knowing who I was: physically, mentally and spiritually. And the woman I am about to become.

As I start to walk, I count my blessings and say a quiet prayer. At the end of the hall, there are two doors: one on each side. Before I can think about pushing a door to show me the way outside, a door opens.

Author's Note

This book is dedicated to the two shoeless girls
I saw at the rest stop. I pray they are okay now.

The following resources are related to the issues of human trafficking and child abuse intervention:

National Human Trafficking Hotline
1-888-373-7888
www.traffickingresourcecenter.org

National Center for
Missing & Exploited Children
24-Hour Call Center:
To report information about a missing or exploited child call the 24-hour Call Center:
1-888-THE-LOST (1-800-843-5678)
Report child sexual exploitation online at
CyberTipline.org

The Hotline telephone numbers and websites are provided with permission from the National Human Trafficking Resource Center (NTRC) with Polaris and National Center for Missing & Exploited Children.

This is for informational purposes only and is not in any way an endorsement of this book by the organizations.

Acknowledgements

I am indebted to countless people for their wisdom and support. The following acknowledgements are not exhaustive. Thank you to the many people who have helped me along the way.

- C.N., my favorite 7-year-old in 2013, former first grader, explaining to me how to write a book, as explained to her by her teacher
- MJ, my Boca Gal, for filling in the New York City details
- Uncle T, for his arrest in Mexico
- My Weight Watcher coaches and friends at the Saturday morning workshops. Go Purple!
- C.S., for all of our adventures and lunches! (Plus meeting a certain green card man!)
- My seventh-grade English teacher, Mrs. Hilton, for assigning us to write a 4 to 7 page book. I forgot to include the dash in my homework notebook and wrote a **47-**page story. My real love of writing had begun and she was my first cheerleader! RIP.
- H.R., who did an amazing job with details and corrections on my first draft!
- A.R., who believed in me when I didn't (after reading yet another draft)
- G-t-D, Couponing Wizard!
- T.G., my favorite blue dress designer.

- For all of the families that I nannied!

- J.W., my favorite holder of secrets

- Though they do not know me (yet!): Oprah Winfrey for her 25 years of shows and "Super Soul Sunday" and guests; All of the ladies of "The View," Jon Stewart and Stephen Colbert, for my nightly laughs; and Ellen DeGeneres, for my afternoon laughs.

- Rachel Hollis: Checked off this goal!

- Dr. J., my editor, and for helping me with the finishing touches

- My kids, who probably thought they'd never see me finish this book after talking about it for so many years.

- My husband, my greatest cheerleader. Thank you for…everything.

About the Author

This is Carol Ann DeLaRosa's debut novel. When she is not writing a novel, she enjoys reading, hiking in the North Carolina mountains, painting, writing her many pen pals, collecting U.S. postage stamps, and, most especially, spending time with her friends and family. She is also an avid bird watcher from her kitchen table.

She lives in Raleigh, North Carolina, with her husband, Mark.

www.carolanndelarosa.com